# Content Warnings

Warning: This book contains explicit sexual content, including pet play, which is only suitable for mature readers, references to past child abuse, homophobic slurs, guns, and attempted suicide.

# Drive

Courtney Maguire

# Other Books by Courtney Maguire

*For those who found strength in unexpected places*

# Chapter 1

U nder the hood of a car, everything makes sense. Gears and wires. Oil and grease. All the parts fit together and just work. Each piece has its own function, a logic. Completely predictable even when damaged. Won't turn over? Check the battery, the wiring, the alternator. Find the broken piece and the whole thing comes alive again, purring and growling and shrugging itself back into action.

I pulled my head out of the engine compartment of a Nissan Altima and flexed my back with a satisfying crack. The owner brought it in complaining of overheating. The repair was a simple one. Just a few hoses needed replacing. I wiped my grease-coated hands and folded my tall frame into the driver's seat. I flicked the key, and the engine turned over easily. I tapped the accelerator and the temperature needle climbed before stopping at normal. I smiled and gave the dash an affectionate pat.

"Good girl."

"Red!" I jumped at a sharp voice from inside the shop. I shut off the Nissan and stepped out to find my boss, Bo, poking his square head into the garage, gesturing for me to join him. Visible through a bank of windows behind him stood a neatly dressed man with long,

1

ink-black hair and a troubled expression. I'd seen him before. Many times, in fact. He drove a silver BMW 5 series sedan, a fine machine and well-suited to a man like him, and he brought it in monthly for regular maintenance.

I always noticed. Not only the car, but the man. How the air changed with his appearance. How, like now, the gears in my head locked up and stopped moving, and all I could do was stare, mesmerized by the flow of his hair around his shoulders, the bow of his lips, his olive skin. He was nothing like the rednecks here in Black Creek. I struggled for a word to describe him. Pretty was what he was. Not in a feminine sense. More in the way you think of a Ferrari 458 as pretty. Sleek and stylish with a touch of ferocity lurking just beneath the shiny topcoat.

"Redmond!"

I jumped again, my eyes jerking back to Bo's irritated face.

"What the hell are you doing? Get in here!"

Face hot, I slammed the car door behind me. I straightened my collar, immediately feeling ridiculous for doing so, and made my way into the shop.

"Mister Itachi," he announced as I stepped through the door, "this is Redmond Cole. He's our finest mechanic. I can assure you he'll have you fixed up in no time."

I nodded without raising my eyes, dirty hands shoved in my pockets. Mr. Itachi. Victor. I knew his name already, had seen it on intake forms and receipts, but unlike the other countless names I encountered daily this one stuck. He shifted nervously, his shiny leather shoes scraping across the shop floor. I lifted my eyes just enough to see his lips curl downward and lowered my head to hide my flush.

"I have a very important meeting in Longview, tomorrow," he said, each word crisp and carefully formed. "It is absolutely imperative it's ready by first thing in the morning."

"Yessir." My tongue stuck to the roof of my mouth, making the words thick.

"Trust me," Bo assured him, slapping me roughly on the back with a meaty hand. "He'll have it ready if he has to work all night."

I frowned and swallowed hard as he gave my shoulder a tight, warning squeeze.

Mr. Itachi clenched and unclenched his hands at his waist, and he released a long sigh. "I guess I'll leave it to you then."

My tongue frozen in place, I nodded again. Bo released his grip on my shoulder and ushered the gentleman out in a fog of reassurances, each one laced with a subtle threat pointed at me.

Heart pounding, palms sweating, I retreated into the garage. I leaned heavily against the Nissan I'd just been working on. My coworker, Lawrence, squinted at me from underneath a Mazda 3, and I pulled myself up straight.

*Goddammit, Red, get a hold of yourself.*

"What is it with that guy?" he said in his three-pack-a-day voice, jabbing his wrench toward the windows.

My stomach clenched. "What do you mean?"

"Bo can't seem to jump high enough when he comes around."

I released a nervous laugh and shrugged. "Money talks, I guess."

Lawrence snorted, disappearing back under the Mazda. Here in Black Creek, there were two classes of people: the obscenely wealthy and everyone else barely scraping by. Like every other East Texas town, we were founded on lumber and natural gas. Those who got in early prospered. Those who didn't worked for them. Generations of people whose fate was determined by the luck of their great-great-grandfathers, though something told me Mr. Itachi's story was different. The silver BMW pulled into the bay next to me, and I peered at it over the Nissan's roof.

"What's wrong with you?" I whispered to myself.

Bo escorted Mr. Itachi to a loaner vehicle, and I approached the BMW as if it were a wounded animal. I inhaled deeply to get the gears moving again, focusing on the machine in front of me. Metal and rubber and glass. Things I understood. But I saw him reflected in every surface. I ran a hand over the curve of the fender, and my face heated. I opened the driver's side door, and the faintly sweet and musky smell of leather and expensive cologne was enough to make me swoon.

With a growl, I forced these distracting thoughts away and gave the ignition a vicious twist. *It's just a car, for fuck sake.* After a brief hesitation, the machine sprang to life in a cacophony of bangs and rattles. I popped the hood, watched the engine tremble in its compartment, and frowned.

"You're a sick girl," I said softly, knocking my knuckles against the engine, "but I can fix you."

Four hours later and I still struggled with the beast, flat on my back underneath the BMW and covered head to toe in grease. The shop had long closed, and with threats of firing and no small amount of bodily harm, even Bo went home, and I was alone with only the clank of metal on metal to keep me company.

"Okay, girl," I said as I tightened the final bolt. "Let's give it a shot."

I slid out from under the car, gave my hands a quick wipe on a shop rag, and slid into the cab. I held my breath and said a little prayer as I turned the key. A slight hesitation before the engine jerked back to life, complaining and grumbling before settling into a steady purr.

"There ya go," I said with a satisfied sigh. I switched the car off, sank back into the seat, and closed my eyes, my long day settling over me like a heavy blanket. A sort of exhaustion that made every-thing soft and dreamlike. I traced the stitching of the leather seats and imagined him sitting here doing the same thing. My eyes cracked open, and I spotted a powder-blue scarf pooled in the passenger seat. My heart skipped a little as I pictured him wearing it, wrapped up to the edge of his pretty lips in it.

"What are you doing?" I muttered to myself as I reached out for the scarf. My face heated up as I fondled the edge. Had his skin touched here? His lips? His breath? I shifted in the seat as my jeans tightened. No, no, no, this couldn't happen here. Anyone could walk in and see.

"This is so fucked." My gaze darted through the windows as I pulled the door fully closed. I dipped my hand into the little pool of fabric and pulled it to my face, letting out a groan as the sweet smell of his cologne enveloped me. Arousal screamed through my veins. My free hand drifted between my legs and squeezed. My hot breath filled the scarf, my smell mixing with his in a way that made my skin burn. How long had it been since I'd been so close to someone? So close, we rubbed off on each other?

I closed my eyes shut tight as a hundred voices swirled around in my head. My pastor's voice declaring homosexuality a sin. My coworkers' casual digs labeling anything less than hypermasculine as gay. The Colonel shouting his judgement: *Disgusting. Pervert. Fag.*

A light, tingly sensation danced across my inner thighs, and when I opened my eyes, Victor Itachi knelt in the floorboard. He pressed his palms to my legs, pushing my knees apart and drifting steadily upward. A little, disbelieving sound slipped past my lips as his long fingers grazed my zipper, pushed my hand out of the way, and tugged it down. My hips jerked as he freed me, and the voices disappeared as he, without ceremony or hesitation, took me into his mouth.

His lips, his full, beautiful lips, were just as soft as I thought they would be. He wrapped them around the head, easing them lower and lower down my shaft in slow, bobbing motions until he had taken me as far as he could go. Hollowing his cheeks, he pulled back in one long stroke, his tongue dragging along the underside of my entire length before plunging back down again, leaving me gasping.

His long hair fell around his face like a shroud, each stroke sending shivers through my hips and abdomen. I reached down and swept back the silken strands, gathering them in my hand and smudging a bit of grease across his cheek. Something about it thrilled me, how I'd dirtied him, and he looked all the more beautiful for it. I gripped his hair and lifted my hips, thrusting myself deeper into his mouth, and his throat shuddered, making me throw my head back and moan.

When I opened my eyes again, he straddled my thighs, naked from the waist down but otherwise dressed as he had been in the shop that afternoon, his cock poking long and hard from under his shirttails. He found the little lever under the seat and threw us back as he rolled his hips over me, pushing his hardness against mine and filling me with sparks.

I blinked, and I was inside him, my hands clutching his hips hard enough to bruise. His head tipped back, his eyes closed. My breath caught as I observed the subtle changes in him. How his face reddened, his eyes clouded with lust, his muscles contracting rhythmically around me as he adjusted to the penetration. I pushed my hips upward and he made the softest of sounds, little more than a sigh, his brow creasing and back arching. I pushed upward again, and he whined, breath quickening, hands balled into fists in my shirt. Again, and he cried out, words thick and slurred, calling my name.

"Red!"

Something exploded inside me at the sound of my name on his lips. I lurched off the seat and pounded myself into him, pressing his back against the steering wheel. Blood on fire, dizzy with the smell of him, my hips snapped and jerked with a will of their own, making the car shake and honking the horn with every stroke. I buried my face in his hair and tasted the salt of his skin. He poured his voice into my ear until the fire inside me grew so hot I could no longer contain it.

When I opened my eyes, I was alone. Panting, I slumped over the steering wheel with my cock in my hand, my pants and shirt stained with the evidence of my perversion. Ears ringing with a voice that never was, head swimming with ghost images, I gathered myself as best I could and slipped out of the car. I still held his scarf in my hand, now soiled with come and grease. I couldn't leave it here. So, I took it with me.

# Chapter 2

The next morning, Mr. Itachi came to fetch his car, which, of course, now ran perfectly. I hid myself away in the darkest corner of the garage and watched as he inspected it, his perfect lips pulling into a smile. He lowered himself into the seat and my throat clenched as if the leather seat held some lingering memory of my actions, all my secrets revealed in the sound of the engine as it turned over.

I breathed a sigh as the car sprang to life, not with an accusation, but the same gentle purr it had the night before. I slouched against the wall and scratched at the two days' worth of whiskers on my chin. I felt haggard. I *looked* haggard. What small part of the night I hadn't spent working I'd spent staring at the powder-blue strip of cloth now wadded into a ball in my laundry hamper. Right next to my greasy coveralls and dirty underwear. Jesus.

The car clicked off and Mr. Itachi's long, lean frame unfurled from the front seat. I flinched as Bo caught my eye and waved me over. "There's no finer mechanic in the city," he touted as I approached. He slapped me so hard on the back my teeth nearly fell out.

"I'm grateful to you, Mr. Cole." My name sounded seductive

on his lips, dark and honey-coated, nothing like the strained cry from my fantasy. I ducked my head, praying the heat crawling up the back of my neck hadn't reached my face. "You must allow me to thank you properly. Let me buy you a drink."

"Oh, that's not—I mean, you don't need—"

"I insist," he said. He dipped his fingers into his breast pocket, retrieved a business card, and held it out to me. "I'm back in town tomorrow afternoon. Give me a call and we'll set something up."

Throat dry, heart doing flips in my chest, I took the card gingerly between two fingers. I allowed my eyes to lift to his hand, drift over his barely exposed wrist, and up his arm to his face. He smiled warmly before swinging the car door open and lowering himself into the front seat.

"You look like shit, Red," Bo said, his gruff voice shaking me out of my stupor.

"Thanks, Boss." I tucked Mr. Itachi's card into my back pocket and turned back toward the garage.

"Why don't you take the rest of the day off?" I stopped short, throwing him a quizzical look over my shoulder. He shrugged and scratched at his close-cropped head. "Save me paying you overtime."

I snorted. I guess that was as close to an *attaboy* as I was going to get.

* * *

I jumped into my rattly 1986 Ford F-150 and made the short drive from the garage to my two-bedroom frame house situated at the edge of the town. Purposely avoiding the overgrown and weed-infested front lawn, I pulled into my driveway and parked in front of the detached garage behind the house. The garage door sat halfway open, the nose of a 1970 Dodge Challenger peeking out from the dark.

My baby. Both my deepest pleasure and the biggest thorn in my side. It was the first car I ever bought with my own money, earned by two years of sweeping floors and cleaning up grease. A hunk of junk the day I bought it, the Challenger represented everything I ever wanted. Freedom built with my own hands. As it turned out, freedom was a bitch, and it ended up sitting in my garage for over a decade. Guts torn out. Skin pockmarked.

I released a long, tired breath and glared at her spotted bumper. One day.

The back door opened on squealing hinges, and I groaned at the state of the kitchen. "Goddammit, Katie." My kid sister. My late night had left her alone to her own devices, and the kitchen looked like a war zone. A sink overflowing with grease-spattered pans and mixing bowls coated with an unidentifiable scum. A skillet sat on the stove, the lid half off and something charred lurking within. I suppose I should have been happy she didn't burn the place down.

I stood for a long moment in front of the sink and poked at the dishes in a half-hearted attempt to clean up. A pile of mail had accumulated on the counter, and I pushed the envelopes around with my fingertip, exposing a bright red stamp across my electric bill. Past Due. I groaned as exhaustion barreled down on me, lending everything a hazy, faraway quality. My mind drifted to the card in my pocket, and I pulled it out. I leaned back against the fridge and let my fingertips graze the linen finish. His name rippled over the surface in glossy ink: Victor Itachi, Esq.

"You can't call him," I grumbled to myself even as wild fantasies crept their way in. I imagined him showing up at my door in his sleek black suit, a single long-stemmed flower in his hand. Not a rose. That would be too basic, too predictable for a man like him. Something exotic like an orchid dripping with little pink blooms. Then, he would lead me by the hand out to his car and hold the door open for me. All of it terribly sweet, terribly romantic, and completely out of my reach.

A wave of loneliness washed over me, and I tossed the card onto the countertop. I'd long given up on relationships like that. Easy and real. My last relationship had been far from easy and certainly wasn't real. A pharmaceuticals salesman I'd met in a bar in Longview. Turned out Black Creek was part of his territory, leading to a series of clandestine meetings in shitty hotels at the edge of town. For a little over a year, we were lovers in three-day stretches exactly twice a month. But if we passed on the street, we were strangers. In this town, tolerance and diversity were dirty words, and people like me were relegated to the shadows. Not even my sister knew.

Secrets were hard to come by in Black Creek, and I had a big one.

I dragged myself out of the kitchen and across the worn brown carpeting to the living room and fell lengthwise onto the sofa. Everything would make more sense after I'd gotten some sleep.

\* \* \*

I awoke to the particular crunch of potato chips. I peeled my face out of the couch cushions and blinked in the direction of the offending noise. Katie kicked the air in front of the matching armchair with long, thin legs, her pale arms wrapped around a bag of Lay's, her cheeks puffed out. Long auburn hair fell wildly about her shoulders, framing a face still girlishly plump. I felt a little twinge in my heart as I noticed a new sharpness to her cheekbones, evidence of her inevitable march toward womanhood. She was sixteen, now. God, help me.

"What time is it?" I asked, scrubbing at my face.

"Four thirty," she answered around a mouthful of chips. "What are you doing home?"

"Bo sent me home early."

"Nice of him."

"Not really," I said, pushing myself upright. "He just didn't want to pay me overtime."

"What a dick," she scoffed with a spray of crumbs.

"Language."

She scowled in my direction, shoving another handful of chips in her mouth. Her eyes were green like her mother's, but that glare came from our father, and it never failed to make my stomach clench. I'd inherited some things from him too—my tall solid build, my square nose, and deep-set eyes—and I wondered if she felt the same shard of apprehension when she looked at me.

"When did you get home?" The crunching abruptly stopped, and she jerked her eyes away from me. "Katie..."

"I didn't skip, okay! We got let out early."

I fell back down onto the couch with a groan, too tired to argue with her. She was a smart girl. Too smart for her own good, in fact, which meant school bored her. When she did attend, she constantly got into trouble, picking on other kids and making the teachers feel stupid. There was no doubt in my mind she would shine if only they challenged her, engaged with her, but she would never get that in a backcountry public school and the nearest private school was at least an hour away in Longview. There's no way I could get her there even if I could afford the tuition.

"Did you hear about Sean Delaney?"

My guts twisted at the mention of his name. Sean Delaney. The heir of a local lumber company and the one and only out gay man in town. Rumor was he'd been disowned for his "lifestyle choices" and sent away to a boarding school in Austin when he was just a teenager. Even as an adult, he'd taken the hint and stayed away, but the death of his father two years ago brought him back.

"What happened?" I asked, sitting up and rubbing the sleep from my eyes.

"Someone spray-painted his car," she answered, wiggling with glee. "Wrote 'fag' across the hood—"

"Katie."

"What! I'm just telling you what it said," she said, throwing up her hands in submission.

"Well, don't act so happy about it," I barked. "People shouldn't be treated that way, no matter who they are, and if I catch you using that kind of language—"

"Geez, you act like I'm the one who spray-painted his car."

I growled and raked my hands through my hair. *Chill out, Red.* I knew she didn't mean to insult me. Just relaying the hottest gossip, but hearing that word come out of her mouth crushed my heart. I wanted her to be better, did everything I could to raise her better, and I was terrified it wasn't enough. How much could I really do when she didn't even know about her own brother? While working fifty hours a week just to keep us afloat?

My stomach rumbled, and I pushed myself off the couch and toward the kitchen. I stopped short at the pile of bills, now open on the counter. I shot an angry look at Katie, and she lowered her eyes, pulling her knees up to her chest.

"I could get a job," she said softly as her young brow creased.

"No. You're going to school."

"I'm just saying—"

"I said, no." I slapped my hand on the counter, sending envelopes skidding across the surface. "You worry about your grades and boys and fucking prom dresses. Let me worry about this."

She nodded, resting her chin on her knees with a pout. Wrinkling my nose, I picked up the mysterious skillet and peered down into it.

"I was trying to make fried chicken."

I rolled my eyes and dropped the pan back onto the stove. "Want a pizza?"

# Chapter 3

I worked the following morning in a daze. I'd slipped Victor Itachi's card into my pocket on the way out, and every time I stuck my hand in, it poked the ends of my fingers. Like a taunt. *Call him, you pussy.* But I couldn't call him. Not after what I'd done in his car. Not if I didn't want the whole town to know what I was. My neck heated at the very thought. How was I supposed to sit across from him, look him in the eye, with that fantasy rolling around in my head? Then again, maybe I needed a dose of reality. Maybe I'd find out he was an insufferable bore with a wife and five kids, and all my romantic ideas would shrivel to dust.

"You okay, Red?" Bo's voice boomed from behind me, startling me so bad I banged my head on the hood of the Chevy I was working on. "You seem a bit more wound up than usual."

"I'm fine, Boss," I grumbled.

"You've got the battery wired backward."

I cursed and yanked the wires free. "Actually, I'm gonna take a break. I need to make a phone call."

I wiped my greasy hands on a rag and ducked into the locker room before Bo could protest. Hands shaking so hard I could hardly manage

14

the combination lock, I opened my locker and grabbed my cell phone. *You're being fucking ridiculous. Just get it over with.* The card in one hand, I carefully punched the number into the phone and hit send.

*Panic set in at the sound of the electronic ring. Fuck, what am I doing? This is stupid. I can't do this I can't do this I can't—*

"Victor Itachi."

*Shit.*

"Oh, um...Mister Itachi." I swallowed hard, my tongue stuck to the roof of my mouth. "This is Red...Redmond...Cole. From the shop. I worked on your—"

"I know who you are, Mister Cole." That honey voice. I could hear him smiling. "I'm glad you called. My evening just opened up."

"Oh. About that...it's not that I don't appreciate—"

"I have reservations at Cafe Dulce for eight o'clock. A business meeting just canceled. Would be a shame to waste it."

Cafe Dulce. Dinner there would cost me a week's pay. "I wish I could, but..."

"Don't worry about the cost. I'll expense it." He chuckled, and it sent vibrations all the way down to my pelvis. "Sorry, but I have to go. See you tonight."

"Mister Itachi—" The line went dead, leaving me staring at a blank screen.

What just happened?

\* \* \*

"Wooooow, look at you. Hot date?"

I scowled at Katie in the mirror as I buttoned the collar on a burgundy dress shirt and ran a comb through my freshly washed hair. I was well overdue a haircut, and no matter what I did, it stuck out over my ears. "Not a date. Just business."

"Business. Right," she said with a disbelieving smirk, pulling off a bite of her Twizzler with a sharp snap. "Who is she?"

"It's not a date."

"Please," she said, rolling her eyes. "I haven't seen you this concerned with your appearance since...well, ever. It's either a date or you want it to be." She thrust the end of her Twizzler at me accusingly. "Spill."

"I told you, it's just business." I pushed past her, avoiding her eyes as I pulled a pair of patent leather shoes from the back of the closet. "We did some last-minute emergency repairs and *he* wants to take me for drinks as a thank-you." She deflated a little, leaning against my door frame. "The place is kind of fancy. I just...don't want to embarrass myself."

She screwed up her face. "Is that normal?"

"Not really."

She sighed and plopped down on the bed next to me as I pulled on my shoes. "It's not because of me, is it? You know...that you don't date."

"What are you talking about?"

She snapped off another bite of her Twizzler and kicked at the empty air. "I've lived with you for three years, and I've never seen you with a girl."

"Katie..."

"You know, your dick will shrivel up if you don't use it once in a while."

"Wow, really?"

She snickered and hopped off the bed to plant a cherry-scented kiss on my cheek.

"Well, you look nice," she said, giving me a reassuring pat on the shoulder.

"Thanks."

\* \* \*

My battered pickup didn't exactly fit in with the Mercedes and BMWs in the parking lot, so I parked on the street a couple of blocks away. Glancing nervously at the little scrap of paper with the address, I navigated my way to Cafe Dulce, arriving about five minutes ahead of our planned meeting time. I took a deep breath, straightening my collar and smoothing the wrinkles from my slacks before slipping through the wide glass doors.

Inside, the place was a jarring mix of light and dark. Black lacquer surfaces reflected bright track lighting in shards of white. I blinked rapidly, my eyes refusing to focus in the confusing play of shadows. A host clad entirely in black materialized behind a podium, stopping me before I got more than two steps in.

"Reservation?" he barked.

"What? Oh, I—I'm not sure..." He arched his eyebrow at me, tapping a manicured fingernail on the surface of the podium. "I'm meeting somebody here."

He jabbed with his pen to a bar to the left of us, a slab of black granite underlit with white LEDs, and shifted his attention to the couple entering behind me. I drifted to a barstool where an equally pretentious bartender quirked his eyebrow at me, wiping down a glass with a rag.

"I'll have...an old-fashioned." I don't know why. Just seemed the right thing to do.

The bartender smirked and set to making my cocktail in the very glass he'd been cleaning. I tapped my feet on the rails and picked at my permanently oil-stained fingernails. When my drink arrived, I downed half of it in one go. Sweet and sharp and bitter all at once.

God, I didn't belong in a place like this. What was I doing here?

"My, my, Mister Cole. You sure clean up nice."

I jumped up out of my barstool, nearly falling over in the process. Victor Itachi stood behind me, looking very sleek in a char-coal-gray suit, his long black hair falling neatly past his shoulders.

The light caught little glints of silver everywhere. Cufflinks, tie-pin, a thick silver band on his thumb.

"Mister Itachi." I choked, blushing as I righted myself.

"Victor, please," he said, waving off my politeness like an annoying gnat. "What are you drinking?"

"Oh, um...old-fashioned."

The corners of his mouth twitched upward as he gestured for the bartender. "Two old-fashioneds, please. Have them sent to my table." I opened my mouth to protest, but the words got stuck when he laid a gentle hand on my elbow and ushered me away from the bar. "Been waiting long?"

"No. I—just got here." Fuck, my hands were sweating. "This place is...nice."

Victor gave an indifferent little shrug and dropped me into a chair at a table for two. The place was nothing but dark corners. Despite all the tables stacked around us, ours felt isolated. Our drinks arrived just as Victor slid into the seat across from me along with a pair of menus which he promptly waved away, instead rattling off a stream of practiced Italian.

"You speak Italian?"

He arched an eyebrow. "That surprises you?"

"It's unexpected, I guess."

"Why's that?"

His eyes narrowed, and I wanted to sink into the floor. "No, I didn't mean—"

"It's an Italian restaurant."

"You're right. I'm sorry." My cheeks burned as if I'd had my nose pressed against a running engine. "I'm an asshole."

Victor sat very still, the silence between us stretching for an eternity.

"I forgive you," he said finally. A slow smile crept across his face. "There aren't many *Itachis* in Black Creek, after all."

I released a nervous laugh as he lifted his glass and touched it to mine. He took a delicate sip, his lips curling softly around the edge of the glass. Mine hit the table with a hollow sound, the only thing left what clung to the ice.

"Tell me about yourself, Mister Cole."

"Redmond," I said, rattling the ice in my glass. "Red."

"Okay. Redmond." He laughed a small, soft laugh. "How long have you been working on cars?"

"Oh, forever," I said with a sweep of my hand. "I started in my first garage when I was sixteen. All I did was sweep floors, but there was this guy there—" I stopped short, choked with a sudden panic that I'd given myself away. Victor simply took another sip of his drink and rested his chin on his hand, eyebrows raised as he waited for me to continue. I drained my glass, pushed it toward the edge of the table, and curled the straw around my finger. "He would let me watch over his shoulder. Taught me things."

"You fell in love with it?"

"Yeah," I said, fighting a burst of warm nostalgia. The truth was, I'd fallen in love with *him*, the first in a long line of intense yet unrequited infatuations. "Yeah, I guess I did."

We both leaned back as a tray of thinly cut meats and hard cheese arrived along with a basket filled with dark bread. The waiter slipped a fresh drink I didn't order under my hand. Victor took one of the loaves and tore off a piece, slathered it with a white cheese, and topped it with a slice of meat before handing the whole assembly over to me.

"Did you order for me?" I asked with an uncomfortable laugh.

"Hope you don't mind."

"I thought this was only drinks."

"Turns out, I'm hungry for more."

I laughed and tried not to wonder if the innuendo was intentional. "What's this?" I asked, taking the bread gingerly between two fingers.

"Pane Toscano Scuro with Burrata and prosciutto."

"I have no idea what you just said."

He laughed. "It's good. Just try it."

"You like to be in control, don't you?"

"In all things," he said with a sly grin. "Try it."

I lifted the bread to my lips and his grin widened. The crust of the bread crunched between my teeth and was surprisingly sweet, complimented nicely by the saltiness of the cheese and slight sharpness of the meat. I rolled the bite around in my mouth, savoring the soft textures.

"Now, taste your drink," he said.

"You're trying to get me drunk, aren't you?" I teased as I lifted my glass. I hummed a note of pleasure as the cocktail hit my tongue. The fruit tasted sweeter, the whiskey warmer, and it went down like honey. "Fuuuuck, that's good," I drawled.

"I'm glad you approve," he said, eyes shining as he loaded up another piece of bread and handed it to me. I flushed a little, embarrassed by my expletive, but too distracted by the magic happening on my tongue to apologize. Not to mention the three old-fashioneds warming my belly. "Can I ask you something, Redmond? Something personal?"

"Ask me whatever you want," I said, swooning as another bite of cheesy heaven exploded in my mouth.

"Are you gay?"

I nearly spat my food in his lap. "I—um—what?"

"It's not a judgement, just a question," he said calmly. "Are you gay?"

It felt like being struck by lightning. My eyes jerked to the faces of the people around us. Did they hear? Did they know? How did *he* know? My heart pounded like a kettledrum.

"You can't—I mean, that's not—"

"Any of my business, I know." He released a small, exasperated sigh. "But I have a proposition—"

"A *proposition?*" I bellowed the word, jumping up from my chair. "What the fuck is this?"

"Sit down, Redmond," he said, firm but calm.

"You thought you could get me liquored up, feed me food I can't pronounce, and then what?"

"Sit." He didn't shout, didn't even raise his voice, but something in his tone changed, sending a shiver through me and strangling off all further argument. His expression went from tranquil, almost disinterested, to sharp as a razor and some deep animal part of my brain recognized it. My third drink hit me hard and fast, and I told myself that was why I sat down. To keep myself from falling. Not because he told me to.

He sighed again, folding his hands primly on the table in front of him. "Forgive my choice of words," he said, his face softening. "What I meant was an invitation. I'm part of a group..."

"Oh, Jesus Christ," I said on the end of an exhale.

"A group of people with, let's say...socially unacceptable tastes." He paused, watching me carefully for a reaction. I threw back the remains of my drink. I'd gone numb at that point. "We get together in a safe place a couple of times a week to explore those tastes."

"So, like a kinky sex club?" I slurred.

Victor shrugged. "It can be whatever you like. Some people just come to be around people like them. Some to get away from the oppression of their boring, vanilla lives. Some just don't want to feel like the biggest freak in the room."

"But mostly sex though, right?" He shrugged, and all I could do was laugh. "Well, fuck me. That was rhetorical."

"We're getting together tomorrow night," he said, flicking a crumb off the tablecloth. "You should come. You don't have to do anything. Just see how it feels."

"Right." I raked my hands through my hair with a groan and pushed away from the table. "Well, Mister Itachi..."

"Victor."

"Thank you for the drinks and the food and the...invitation, but I think I'll call it a night."

I stumbled a little as I got out of the chair. Victor didn't react, simply pinched off a piece of bread in his same disinterested fashion, but the corners of his mouth pulled slightly downward.

"If you change your mind, you know how to reach me," he said, pushing the bread into his mouth.

## Chapter 4

"Front desk!" I called from flat on my back underneath a Toyota Camry as the front desk buzzer cut through the air, reflecting off concrete and metal. A short silence followed, filled only with the rattle of my socket wrench, before it picked up again more insistently than before. "For fuck sake, somebody gonna get that?"

I scooted back just enough to poke my head out from under the car. Randy and Lawrence leaned against the tailgate of an F-150, glaring toward the bank of windows separating the garage and the front office, their faces a mixture of disgust and morbid curiosity.

"Guys." Their eyes jerked down to me.

"It's him," Randy said, his nose wrinkled.

"Who?"

"That queer."

My mouth went dry and I looked up toward the windows. Sean Delaney. He paced the front office like a nervous animal, his sandy-blond hair sticking out as if he'd been tugging on it. Outside sat his navy-blue Prius, the word "FAG" scrawled across the hood in bright yellow paint.

He hit the buzzer again and it rang through the shop. "So, you're just going to ignore him?"

"It's that queer," Lawrence repeated. As if it was an answer.

"He's a customer, just like anybody else."

Lawrence scoffed. "'Cept he ain't like everybody else."

"And, what, you think it's contagious?" My coworkers' faces pinched. "Fucking unbelievable," I grumbled as I rolled out from under the car.

Sean's back was to me as I entered the office and he jumped a little at the sound of the door. He was a small man, a little on the short side with a slim, boyish physique, and he trembled like a cornered rabbit.

"Sorry about the wait," I said. "Can I help you?"

"I...um..." He wrapped his arms around himself, his gaze darting around the room as if in search of an exit. He paused a moment, taking a deep breath before pulling himself up straight. "My car was vandalized. Can you fix it?"

I let out a long breath. I moved toward the front window and he moved back, keeping the distance between us constant.

"That it?" As if I didn't know.

He nodded, lips pressed into a thin line.

"You know, this isn't a body shop," I said gently.

"Well, I've been to every body shop in town," he said, his voice trembling and eyes pinched, frustrated tears brewing just beneath the surface. My stomach twisted and I thought of Randy and Lawrence's expression. This fucking town.

I squinted at the car through the window and scratched at the stubble on my chin. Bo wouldn't like this. Randy and Lawrence would certainly give me shit for it.

Fuck those guys.

"Okay," I said on the tail end of an exhale. Sean's eyes widened in surprise and relief. "I know a trick or two that might work. I can't guarantee your paint job..."

"Fair enough," he said, nodding enthusiastically. "As long as I don't have to look at that word anymore."

"Pull her around. I'll meet you in the garage."

My heart broke a little as he ran out of the door and jumped in his car. I grabbed a clipboard off the desk and ducked back into the garage where Randy and Lawrence stared, jaws agape.

I shot them an icy glare as I passed. The Prius slid almost silently into the garage, its hybrid electric engine whirring. Sean got out and threw a wary glance in my coworkers' direction.

"Don't worry about them," I said under my breath as I handed him the clipboard and he visibly relaxed. Thin brows lowered over his eyes as he focused on the form, the smallest crease forming between them. My eyes followed the line down the bridge of his long nose, across his high cheekbones, along the square of his jaw.

"Thank you for this," he said, his eyes flicking up at me. They were green.

"It's my job," I said with a shrug, croaking around a thickness in my throat.

"Even so." He handed the clipboard back to me with a grateful smile and my cheeks warmed.

I cleared my throat. "It'll probably be a couple days. I'll call you when it's ready."

He nodded. "Guess I'll be taking the bus for a while."

A familiar expression settled over his face as he searched up the street for the nearest bus stop. Fear tinged with exhaustion and it made my bones ache. I glanced over my shoulder at Randy and Lawrence, their heads tucked back under the hoods of their respective cars but obviously still listening, and a tingle ran down my back.

"I could...give you a ride."

"Oh, you don't have to..." he started, but his eyes lit up with hope.

"It's no big deal. We do it for clients all the time and I need a break, anyway."

He nodded, and after he'd grabbed a few things from the back seat, we headed out to my truck. Randy's eyes burned a hole in my back, but I ignored it, hopped into the cab, and reached across to unlock the passenger door. Sean pulled himself in, struggling a little with the height, and settled into the seat with a nervous shimmy.

We traveled most of the way in silence, my grip on the steering wheel white-knuckle tight. This was a mistake. Just the thought of Randy and Lawrence speculating about me and Sean made me queasy. I ran our short conversation over and over in my head, analyzing every word and mannerism. Did I stand too close? Smile too long?

I snuck glances at Sean as he watched businesses and houses pass. His expression wavered as we passed a couple holding hands and a strange, amorphous guilt passed through me. He was alone, or at least he thought he was, in a hostile land where everyone seemed happy but him. Where a life and love felt just out of reach. I knew that feeling, struggled with it every day, the only difference was I hid in the shadows. I wore a mask against the hate, keeping everyone at arm's length for fear they'd see through me. Part of me admired his bravery. The other part wondered if it was really worth it.

He pointed me into a long driveway which led to a southwestern-style home, all-natural stone and red tile roofs. Wide windows and an arched entryway faced a lush green lawn. I put my pickup truck into park, throwing us into an awkward silence.

"Nice place."

"It's not really mine. It was my father's," he said with a shrug. "Did you want to come in? The least I can do is offer you a drink."

"I've...gotta get back to work."

"Right." He paused a moment, his hand on the door and a furrow in his brow. "Well, thanks...um..."

"Red."

"Like the color?" he asked, arching his eyebrow.

"Short for Redmond." I scratched the back of my neck. "It's an old family name. I sort of hate it."

"Oh, I see." He smiled and this time it almost reached his eyes. "Thanks, Red."

\* \* \*

I drove around for half an hour before returning to work, rattling with nervous energy. Was I polite? Was I too polite? Did anyone see me with him? Did they know? Did *he* know? Did he like me? I should have gone in for a drink. God, what would have happened if I'd gone in for a drink?

The thought sent me into a tailspin of fantasies that made me flush. This was ridiculous. One interaction and I reacted like a horny teenager. The last thing I needed was to be outed by wandering eyes or a stray hard-on.

Or jacking off in a customer's car.

I groaned as Victor Itachi's face flashed before my eyes. His proposition rang in my ears. *I'm part of a group...* How long had it been since I'd last been with somebody? I didn't even want to think about it. I was doing just fine before I met him with his long hair and his pretty lips. Now, a need simmered beneath my skin and made me sweat. *You know, your dick will shrivel up if you don't use it once in a while.* Sitting in the parking lot of the garage, I pulled my phone out of my pocket and stared at his number.

Sean Delaney wouldn't have this problem. If he wanted to get laid, he'd just visit the next town over where there was an actual gay bar and have his pick. I'd visited once or twice myself and skulked in a corner, too much of a coward to even talk to anyone.

Fuck.

Before I could chicken out, I tapped out a quick text message.

*Okay, I'm in.*

I dropped the phone in my lap, shriveling in embarrassment. "What are you doing? This is insane," I said, resting my head on the steering wheel until the phone vibrated in my lap.

*Good. Tonight, 9:00,* he responded, followed with an address.

* * *

What does one wear to an orgy?

In the end, I decided to go as I was: a T-shirt with a Pennzoil logo on the chest and a pair of jeans. Strangely afraid of my truck being spotted, I took the bus, arriving at the specified address just a few minutes before nine. A sports bar, sparsely populated by big dudes in football jerseys, gathered in a knot around a big-screen TV. A mecca of heteronormativity. I stared through the big plate window rimmed with neon, sweat forming on the back of my neck. I'd been here a hundred times. Was there some backroom, a seedy basement, a hidden door opened by a secret handshake I wasn't aware of before?

The chirp of a car horn made me jump, and I turned to see Victor's BMW stopped on the curb. He rolled down the window, a smile curling his lips.

"You're on time. Good." He jerked his head toward the passenger side. "Get in."

"But I thought..." I tossed a confused glance over my shoulder at the bar.

"You thought we'd have a drink?" he asked, an amused glint in his eye.

"I think I might need one."

He responded with a silent laugh. He rolled up his window but didn't get out. I shuffled my feet, shoved my hands in my pockets, pulled them out again. Air brakes hissed as a bus pulled into the stop up the street. I could just get on. Go back to my life and pretend this never happened.

Then I thought of Sean Delaney. His tired look. I got in the car.

Black Creek was one of half a dozen small towns clustered together like spokes on a wagon wheel. Victor took us past the city limits and turned down a long, winding driveway lined with cars, stopping in front of what looked like a plantation house situated in the wheel's hub. Tall Roman columns fronted the two-story building, framing a punch-card pattern of windows that pierced the evening gloom with shafts of bright-white light. Manicured hedges trimmed the plush lawn, giving the impression of class, as if we were attending the coming out of a debutante rather than...

....whatever this was.

Victor slipped the BMW into an open space between an Aston Martin and a battered Chevy pickup and cut off the engine. The sudden silence made my heart race and my mouth go dry. He'd spent the drive giving me the basics of what to expect, but I couldn't hear him over my heart pounding in my ears. *Am I really doing this?* Victor watched me, sharp eyes like pinpricks on the back of my neck.

"Remember, you don't have to participate in anything that makes you uncomfortable," he said sternly. "Many choose to simply observe their first time. There's no judgement, here."

I nodded, eyes never leaving the squares of light above. Shadows moved behind gauzy curtains, and my mind twisted them into all sorts of shapes. Victor touched my arm, and I jumped.

"Ready?" he asked, the corners of his mouth turning up in a reassuring smile. I took a deep breath, wiping my sweaty palms on my jeans.

"Yeah, okay."

His door clicked open and I followed suit, shoes crunching on the white gravel driveway. He appeared beside me, giving me a little pat on the shoulder before leading the way toward the house. We climbed two steps onto a wide porch past a man and a woman standing very close together, smoking fragrant cigarettes. They gave us a curious look as we passed, and the woman whispered something in the man's ear that made him chuckle.

"Wait." I stopped short as adrenaline stabbed my heart into an irregular rhythm. Victor half turned, his eyebrow arched in my direction. "W-what if..."

"What if what?"

"If somebody sees me? Recognizes me?" I took a step backward, bumping into the column behind me. "I—I can't—"

"Relax, Redmond," he said with a chuckle. "This is a place built on trust. Besides, if someone sees you here, then they're here too."

I swallowed hard around my sandpaper tongue. "So, trust built on mutually assured destruction."

The corners of his mouth quirked. "Something like that."

The wide oak door was fitted with a small silver knocker, and Victor plucked it up with two fingers. He gave it a quick strike. The door opened a crack, and Victor flashed a thin plastic card resembling a hotel room key. The door opened wider, revealing a man with a neck as thick as my waist. His eyes flicked over Victor's shoulder to me and narrowed slightly before he stepped aside.

My breath caught at the grandeur of the place. The entryway opened into a wide, marble-tiled foyer flanked by three rooms, two on the left side and one on the right, and a staircase worthy of the *Titanic* leading up to the second floor. A round, bear-clawed table stood in the center of the room, its top neatly adorned with an assortment of collars, harnesses, and leather leashes. The only hint of what was really going on within.

Victor wrapped his fingers around my elbow, pulling me closer to him as he pointed to each room in turn. "Men looking for men, women looking for women, and—" He hesitated a moment, his finger lingering on the last room to the right. "—pretty much anything else. Rooms upstairs are key-access only, so if you're looking for something more private, you have to be invited."

"How do you know if you're invited?" I asked, struggling to keep my voice even. The corners of Victor's mouth quirked upward again.

"They'll give you a key."

I swallowed hard and my stomach did a flip. Victor gave my arm a squeeze before releasing it, snatching a thin leather leash from the table, and heading into one of the parlor rooms. Men looking for men.

*Jesus, what am I doing?*

Sweat gathered along my hairline as I followed. The parlor was just a parlor like any other, lined with oversized armchairs and plush leather sofas. About a dozen men lounged among them, some sitting primly with legs crossed and sipping from wineglasses, others draped over piles of pillows like concubines. A lithe young man with heavily painted eyes perked up at our entrance, jumping up from where he lay curled in an armchair, and threw himself into Victor's arms.

"Victor! You're here! I've been so lonely without you," he whined, wrapping his thin arms around Victor's neck and pulling him into a heated kiss. Victor returned it easily. and something inside me clenched. The boy's cat-eye lashes fluttered in my direction, and he separated from Victor with a pout. "Ohhhh, you've brought a friend. Does this mean you don't want to play with me?"

"Don't be silly," he said, scratching him behind the ear. The boy leaned into it, tipping his head back and exposing a thick leather collar. A silver tag dangled from a ring just to the left of his Adam's apple engraved with an extravagant monogram: *VI*.

"This is Redmond," Victor continued, gesturing with his nose in my direction. "Redmond, this is Toby." He hooked his finger in the young man's collar and gave it a sharp tug. "He's new here, so be polite."

The boy's mouth pulled into a long grin, and his hazel eyes flashed as they raked over me, examining me down to my toes. His tongue flicked over his teeth, and I got the impression he wanted to take a bite out of me.

"He's cute. Can he play with us?"

Victor hesitated and Toby bounced on his toes, nuzzling his ear and whining. Victor's eyes slid in my direction, sending a chill down my spine. I tried to respond, but my tongue stuck to the roof of my mouth.

"Maybe next time," he said coolly though his gaze was heated. Toby pouted a little before nudging Victor's eyes back to him, curling the loose end of the leash in his fingers. I swallowed hard as he pushed his nose inside Victor's jacket and pulled the little card out of the inside pocket with his teeth.

"Think you'll be all right on your own for a little while, Redmond?" Victor asked without looking at me, his voice husky.

"I—um—yeah...sure." The corners of his lips quirked, and he snapped the leash onto the boy's collar before leading him out of the parlor and up the stairs to a private room.

I released the breath I'd been holding and, a little dizzy, found my way to an open seat. A deep leather sofa curled around me as I fell into it. I ran my hand over my eyes and tried not to think about what Victor and Toby were doing. About the little monogrammed charm hanging from Toby's collar. Tried not to think about what it all meant.

The sofa shifted underneath me, and I peeked around my fingers at a couple of men cozied up on the other end. The one nearest me appeared to be a businessman, wearing well-pressed trousers and a long-sleeved button-up shirt open at the collar, his jacket slung over the back of the couch a few inches away. A pair of long, mostly bare legs lay across his lap and he dragged his fingertips over a well-defined thigh, teasing at the edge of very short, very tight athletic shorts.

Eyes peeked around the businessman's shoulders, and I jerked mine away. A rush of heat flooded my face and crawled down my neck. I had no idea what the etiquette was in a place like this or if there even was one. A little giggle came from their direction, and when I glanced their way again, both pairs of eyes were pinned on me.

The businessman smiled and pulled his partner, a lean, muscular man with sun-bleached hair and a deep tan, further into his lap. A surfer if I had to guess by the Hurley logo on his open Hawaiian shirt. Without taking his eyes off me, the businessman let his head fall back and his partner trailed open-mouthed kisses down his neck, the surfer's toes curling as he palmed him roughly through his shorts.

My eyes jerked to the other patrons as their groping intensified. They all seemed oddly unaffected with the exception of an older man planted in an armchair, openly gawking with his hand shoved in the front of his jeans. I recognized him. The manager of a family-owned grocery store in Black Creek.

*I can't do this.*

My skin went cold and an electric burst of adrenaline sizzled through my chest. Choking on floral air freshener and the underlying stink of sex, I leaped from the couch and hurtled headlong out of the parlor and toward the front door. The burly doorman saw me coming and, with a wry smile on his lips, opened the door just in time to send me tumbling out.

# Chapter 5

I made it as far as the bottom porch step before I realized I was stuck. I could call a cab, but I didn't even have an address to give them. I swung my head up and down the street searching for landmarks, but the whole property was surrounded by hedges and thick darkness.

With a defeated sigh, I dropped down onto the bottom step, elbows on knees and head in hands. When I closed my eyes, I saw the couple on the couch. Blood rushed to my skin, my cheeks, my cock even as my mind screamed a warning. Such open displays of sexuality should have made me feel safe. We were the same. I wouldn't have to hide here. But spotting a familiar face had triggered a sharp panic in me. I felt perverse, like everything the Colonel told me I was, and my throat tightened with the impulse to vomit.

"You okay?" a female voice asked from behind me. I lifted my head and glanced over my shoulder. The same woman we passed on the way in stood at the top of the stairs. Lithe figure, long blonde hair, a cigarette pinched between her fingers. She leaned against the post drunkenly as she gazed down on me with hooded brown eyes.

"Fine," I answered, gaze dropping to the grass under my feet. The stairs creaked as she stumbled down them and sat next to me.

"Everyone freaks out a little their first time," she said with a sigh bordering on nostalgia. "It's natural, I guess. We've been told our whole lives what to do, how to be, who to fuck even if our bodies are telling us different. Then you come here and realize it was all bullshit. Screws with your worldview a little, ya know?" She paused and took a long pull off her cigarette. "So, what's your deal? Gay, right?"

I flinched, fists clenched between my knees. Even here, it was hard to admit my truth so openly. "Yeah. You?"

"P-and-P." I shot her a confused look and she laughed. "Party and play." She shifted in her seat, dipping her manicured fingers into the pocket of her tight jeans and pulling out a baggie full of pills. "One of these will send you to the moon. Makes everything more intense. Wanna try?"

"Everything's intense enough, thanks."

She smirked and shoved the pills back into her pocket. "You came with Victor, right?" she asked, sucking in a stream of air between her teeth. "He's delicious. Not a soul in this house that doesn't want a piece of him. You're very lucky."

"How's that?"

"He picked you," she said, nudging me with her shoulder. "Means he likes you."

"Funny, since the first thing he did was run off with someone else." Something prickled inside me. Jealousy? *God, I need a hobby.*

"Let me guess. Toby?" She released a barking laugh. "He's just a lapdog. Victor doesn't like Toby near as much as he likes how much Toby likes him. He's giving you time to adjust is all."

"It doesn't matter," I said, raking my hands through my hair. "I don't think I'll be coming back."

"Famous last words."

She kept me company on the step until Victor emerged about

half an hour later, a flush darkening his cheeks and a looseness to his steps. He stopped on the step beside me and she shuffled away without a word, throwing me a wink from behind his back.

"How are you doing, Redmond?" he asked, leaning back against a post.

"A little overwhelmed, honestly." I stood and leaned against the post opposite him, keeping a wide distance between us. I could smell it, whatever he'd done with Toby, and it made my stomach turn. "I'm sorry, but I don't think this is for me."

He released a long breath through his nose, the corners of his mouth pulling downward. "That's a shame," he said softly. "I guess I'll take you home then."

* * *

"What the fuck is that cocksucker's car doing in my garage!"

I didn't even register Bo's words until he slapped his hand on the hood of Sean's car. I jumped, nearly spilling the can of acetone I'd been using to work the spray paint off the surface. I hadn't slept all night, plagued with dreams of what I'd seen at the plantation house. The image of that couple played on a loop in my mind, each repetition more twisted than the last. Victor's face superimposed onto the businessman and the surfer became Sean Delaney.

"Sorry, Bo," I grumbled, "I didn't realize we were in the business of turning away paying customers."

"We don't serve his kind, here."

"And what kind is that?" *Control yourself, Red.*

His face twisted and turned beet red. "This is a family establishment. I won't be offending my loyal customers with this...this..." He gestured wildly at the car, spitting with disgust. "Just get it out of here."

Family establishment. Code for "no gays allowed."

"Look at it this way," I said, taking a deep breath. "He took it to every body shop in town, and no one would work on it. You can mark up the work as much as you want. You know he has the money, and it's not like he can take it anywhere else."

Bo screwed up his face and crossed his arms tightly over his barrel chest. Guilt knotted in my stomach. I was encouraging him to gouge a desperate man. But no matter how backward and bigoted Bo could be, he was a businessman first, and it was only a matter of time before the dollar signs in his eyes won out.

"Fine," he spat, "but it is your lowest priority. You will work on it in your down time only and it will be covered at all times, got it?"

"Got it, boss."

"Wrap this up. I've got Missus Elliot coming in for an oil change in ten minutes."

Bo stomped off back to his office. Randy and Lawrence snickered at me from across the garage and I rolled my eyes as I tossed a tarp over the Prius. Bo spent the rest of the day loading me down with every scrap of work he could find, down to sweeping the floors, to keep me from working on it. In the end, I was only able to squeeze out about a half hour. It would take a year to clean up at this rate.

I had to call Sean.

While my coworkers closed up, I slipped into the front office to use the phone. A strange fluttering started in my stomach as I called up his information and punched in his number. *It's just business, for fuck sake.*

He picked up on the second ring. "Hello?"

"Mister Delaney. This is Red...from the shop."

"Red!" He sounded genuinely pleased to hear from me. "Don't tell me you're finished already."

"I'm afraid not." My voice cracked and I cleared my throat. "Turns out we're a little backlogged here..."

"Oh."

"Might take longer than I expected."

"I see." He was silent for a long time. When he spoke again, his voice was softer. "Did you get into trouble?"

"A little." For some reason, I didn't want to lie. "No big deal."

"Do you fish?"

"Excuse me?"

"I know a place. Kind of my secret spot. You can pull catfish out of the river as big as your arm." He paused a moment, and I pictured that little wrinkle forming in his brow. "Wanna go?"

The fluttering in my stomach turned into full-on somersaults. Fishing with Sean Delaney? The fear that plagued me my whole life rose up so fast it choked me.

"I'm not, like, asking you on a date or anything," he said with a dry laugh.

"Oh, good." I tried to make it sound teasing, but the relief was audible.

"You seem like a good person, is all. You may have noticed I'm short on friends."

"I don't have any tackle or anything."

"That's okay. I've got you covered."

There was a long silence. I picked at a loose piece of Formica on the desk, my mind a tangle. The idea of having a friend, a real one, was intoxicating. Someone I could be open with, could talk to without fear of being found out and ostracized. But being associated with him was a risk in itself.

"Yeah, okay." The words were out of my mouth before I even realized I'd made a decision.

"Great! When do you get off work?"

"About now."

"Pick me up?"

"You're just using me for my truck, aren't you?" I said, a smile teasing at my lips.

"Totally." He laughed. "Half an hour?"

"See you then."

# Chapter 6

After a quick call to my sister to let her know I'd be home late, I finished closing up and headed straight to the Delaney house. Sean was waiting on the porch when I pulled up, a pair of fishing poles in one hand and a tackle box in the other. He met me in the drive, smiling as he tossed the tackle into the back, and it lit up his whole face. It was like looking at a different person, the graceful, confident way his lean body moved as he pulled himself up into the cab.

"Hey," he said.

"Hey." I shifted in my chair, hands wrapped tight around the steering wheel. "So, where to?"

"Just go back to the main road and head east."

I nodded and the truck lurched as I threw it into gear. We traveled mostly in silence with the exception of a few directions, but it was a different silence than the day before. Lighter, gentler, and I relaxed into it as the lights of town faded in my rearview.

He pointed me down a dirt road canopied by tall oaks that opened up into a clearing right on the riverbank. The low-hanging sun gave everything a soft quality. Gold light skipped over the surface of the snaking river as far as the eye could see in either direction. Cattails and marsh weeds grew tall in the shade of the trees along the bank, the relatively still water creating a haven for mayflies and other small insects.

I backed the truck up to the water and we both hopped out. He reached over into the back as I dropped the tailgate, fetching both rods. He shoved one into my hands, laughing at my lost expression.

"Don't tell me your dad never took you fishing."

I scowled down at the reel and its mess of string. "No, he was never really into this stuff."

"Not much of an outdoorsman?"

"Not much of a dad."

Sean's expression fell a bit, his eyes softening. "Well, it's easy. You just drop the hook in the water and let the fish come to you."

I pinched the hook between my fingers, sure there was more to fishing than that, as he flipped open the tackle box lid and retrieved a Styrofoam container. "Good God, man, what is that smell?" I asked when he peeled off the lid, hitting me in the nose with a sharp, slightly rotten odor.

"Chicken livers. Want a taste?" he teased, lifting the container and wafting it in my direction. I grimaced and stifled a gag, clapping a hand over my mouth and nose. "Catfish are scavengers. Stinkier the bait, the better."

I watched in horror as he dipped his fingers into the dark, slimy mass and pulled out a congealed wad of meaty tissue. He plucked the hook out of my fingers and shoved the liver over the barb.

"I can't believe you're touching that."

He scoffed. "You all think I'm some kind of gentrified city-folk," he drawled, leaning into his southern accent, "but you forget, I grew up on this river."

"So did I, and I'm not sticking my hand in there."

"Well, that's just right unmanly," he said with a wink. He went back to the tackle box, fished out a red-and-white bobber, and fastened it to my line. Heat rushed to my face as he laid his hands over mine on the rod and tugged me into casting position. "Hold your thumb on this button on the reel, give the rod a little flick like this," he said, his hand wrapped around my wrist, "then let go. Aim for just at the edge of those weeds."

He stepped back and set to baiting his own hook and I flushed with a rush of self-consciousness. "Ah, shit," I cursed as I released the button too late, landing the hook on dry land down river. He laughed and it sent a shiver up my back.

"It's okay. Just reel it in and give it another try."

Grumbling, I reeled the line back in. The stinky bait skipped up the shoreline back to the end of my pole. I took a deep breath and tried again, this one landing in the water but still well off the mark. Sean clapped before casting his own line, the lure dropping gently into the very edge of the weeds.

"You've done this before."

"Once or twice," he returned with a grin.

"Now, what?"

He hopped up onto the tailgate and gave the space beside him a pat. "Now, we wait."

Sean leaned back on one arm, his other hand wrapped loosely around the rod with a finger resting on the line. He closed his eyes and just breathed the open air. He seemed so at home here, I struggled to picture him in a city, surrounded by concrete and glass.

"Just ask," he said without opening his eyes.

"What do you mean? Ask what?" I asked, flustered.

"Whatever it is you've been sitting on this whole time." He opened one eye and peered at me out of the corner of it.

"I...haven't been—"

"You have." Both eyes were open, now, and they gleamed in the fading light. "If we're going to be friends, we can't have anything hanging between us. So, spill."

"I don't want to offend..."

"You won't," he said with a dry laugh. "I've developed a high tolerance for the shittiness of people."

"Okay..." I took a deep breath, licked my dry lips, wiped my sweaty hands on my jeans. "Do you ever regret it?"

"Regret what?"

"Being...you know..."

"What? Gay?" He released a barking laugh. "Well, it's not like I picked it."

"No, I mean..." What did I mean? "Do you regret people knowing? Coming out or...whatever. Just seems like it would be easier..."

"Easier?" he scoffed. "No."

"But you're a pariah. The whole town hates you. Your own family disowned you."

"Well, since you put it like that—"

"I'm serious."

"Being in the closet is like being one of those mascots you see at football games. Some kid running around in a big chicken suit or something. On the outside, they look like they're having fun, running around making people laugh. But inside, they're sweating and tired and all they want to do is take that suit off."

"That makes absolutely no sense."

"No. I don't regret it," he said firmly, pinning me with his eyes. "Leaving this town was the best thing I could have done. Did I miss my family? Did it hurt that my father, even on his deathbed, didn't want to see me? Yes. But I got to be myself. Austin's not perfect, but there's a supportive community there."

A thrill ran through me, making the small hairs on my arms stand on end. What would it be like to have people who knew me, really knew me, and accepted me for what I was? Someone to guide me when I got lost. Someone to comfort me when I was hurting. A place safe from the world's judgement.

"I had a couple of boyfriends, one who was good to me, one who wasn't." He sniffed, his eyes drifting back out over the water.

"They may not have all been good experiences, but they were real. Had I stayed, I may have had the privilege of my father's name, but it would have been a lie."

"Like the mascot pretending he's having fun?"

"I just wanted out of the damn chicken."

I blew out a long breath. How many times had I been tempted to let go of my secrets, to throw my middle finger up to the whole damn town and their conservative bullshit? But it wasn't just me anymore. I had my sister to think of. I might be willing to put up with the hate and bigotry, but to throw it on her would be unfair. If my house became unlivable, she would have nowhere else to go.

Except back to him.

"So, what about you?"

I jerked, making the floater at the end of my line wobble. "What about me?"

"What's your story?" he asked, the corner of his mouth lifting as he leaned slightly toward me.

"Oh. No story."

"Come on," he said, nudging me with his shoulder. "Everyone has a story. Married? Divorced? Illegitimate children?"

"Never married. No kids. Well, not exactly. My kid sister lives with me," I answered, scratching the back of my neck. "She's sixteen."

"Oof, tough age," he said with a grimace.

"Na, she's a good kid. Too smart for her own good, sometimes, but a good kid."

"So...is it because of your father..."

My shoulders dropped a notch. "Yeah. Colonel Cecil Redmond Cole, Navy Retired." I scoffed. "He's ex-military. Tough, ya know? And, completely unforgiving. I grew up thinking, *believing*, there was something wrong with me." My hands clenched around the fishing rod. "I moved out when I was fifteen. Katie was just a baby. I thought she'd be okay. I was so sure it was me who was the problem. Then, thirteen years later, I get this call from the sister I hardly know. She's desperate, scared, just like I was. I couldn't just leave her there, ya know?"

Sean nodded, his eyes pinched and glistening in the fading light. An embarrassed flush heated my cheeks and I turned my face away.

"I'm sorry. I shouldn't have dumped that on you," I said with a dry laugh. "I just...I don't have a lot of friends either."

"Don't be sorry," he said, smiling warmly. He laid a gentle hand on my knee, sending a burst of warmth through my whole body. "You *are* a good person, Red."

A car horn burst through our little bubble. Panic sliced through me. I dropped the fishing rod and jumped off the tailgate. As if Sean's hand on my leg had turned red-hot.

"I'm sorry. I...um..." My heart pounded in my ears. My tongue stuck in my mouth. I swallowed in an effort to get it moving again. "I...have to go."

"What? What do you mean?" he asked, dropping off the tailgate and taking a step toward me. "Red, what just happened?"

"Nothing. I just...my sister—" I took a step back, putting the truck bed between us. I flinched at the rumble of a diesel engine just on the other side of the trees.

"You don't want to be seen with me."

A statement, not a question, and it knocked the wind out of me. *God, I'm no better than the rest of them.* I didn't look at him, couldn't, and the disappointment flowed off him like water.

"Can we just go?" I said, an unspoken plea in the words. *Don't bring me into this with you.*

"Yeah, okay."

# Chapter 7

"**E**arth to Redmond." Katie snapped her fingers in front of my nose, and I jumped, spilling the spoonful of cereal hanging halfway between my mouth and the bowl. "What the hell's the matter with you, today?"

"Nothing's wrong with me," I grumbled, shoving what was left on the spoon into my mouth.

"Bullshit."

"Language."

"You've been moping around like someone stole your puppy," she said, narrowing her eyes at me. "What gives?"

"Nothing *gives*," I said. "Just didn't sleep well, is all."

The truth was, I didn't sleep at all. I replayed my brief interaction with Sean Delaney over and over in my head as if I could change it, my thigh super-heated by an innocent touch, a supportive touch. I flopped around on the bed, sweating, my stomach in knots. One friendly gesture and I reacted like a kid about to get busted for making out under the bleachers. Worse, like I was ashamed of who I was under there with.

"Aren't you late for school or something?" I asked, shaking the thoughts from my head.

"Yeah, about that..." Katie's eyes dropped to the table and she pulled her lip between her teeth. "I got suspended."

"For fuck sake, Katie—"

"Language," she sneered.

"What did you do?"

"I didn't do anything," she said, slapping her hands on the table. "It's not my fault my teachers are incompetent."

"Katie—"

"All I did was correct my Chem teacher when she made a mistake."

"You can't do that," I said, leaning over the table toward her. "You can't keep contradicting your teachers."

"Even when they're wrong?"

"Yes, even when they're wrong," I snarled.

"What am I supposed to do?" she asked, cheeks red, eyes tearing.

"You shut your mouth and do as you're told."

I regretted the words the moment they left my tongue. She jerked back in her chair, mouth falling open. "Listen and obey. Like a good little soldier." Her mouth twisted, and her eyes overflowed. "Jesus, Red, you're my brother. You're supposed to be on my side."

"Katie—"

"You sound just like Dad."

I reeled as if she'd struck me. She shoved away from the table, the milk sloshing out of both our bowls, and stomped out of the room. The slamming bedroom door rang like a gunshot. I didn't move, nailed to the spot by my own inadequacy.

*You are a good person, Red.*

Yeah, right.

I had to go to work. I pushed myself out of the chair in the kitchen only to fall heavily into the couch in reach of my work boots. I'd just pulled them on when her door creaked open behind me. I glanced over my shoulder to find Katie, eyes puffy, face pinched, hands bunched in the hem of her shirt.

"Come here," I said with a sigh and a wave of my hand. She shuffled toward me on the balls of her feet like a child and threw herself down on the couch beside me, looping her skinny arms around my neck.

"I'm sorry, Red," she sniffled. "I'm sorry. I didn't mean it."

"I know," I said, pulling her into my chest and kissing her hair. "I'm sorry too."

"You're a way better dad than he is and you're just my brother. Not even a full brother."

"There's no half or full," I said sternly, taking her face in my hands and forcing her to look at me. "You're my sister and I'm on your side. Even if I mess up sometimes, I'll always be on your side. We're a team. Got it?"

"Got it." She smiled up at me through her tears, the little girl I missed growing up, and it pained me. I swept her auburn waves out of her face and kissed her forehead before pushing her upright.

"I've gotta go to work. Think you can manage to not burn the house down?"

"I'll do my best," she said with a laugh.

"Want me to try talking to your teacher?"

Her eyes dropped and she shrugged with one shoulder. A noncommittal gesture that meant yes but didn't give up any ground. I pinched her nose, bringing back her smile.

"See you, kiddo."

"See you, brother."

\* \* \*

The sun was out, and the wind had shifted, bringing in a wash of cooler air that took the edge off the summer heat. I decided to take advantage of the relatively temperate day and eat my lunch on the tailgate of my truck. In an effort to make up for the trouble at school and our subsequent spat, Katie brought me a rather pleasant bag lunch consisting of a ham and cheese sandwich, a baggie of baby carrots, and a Little Debbie snack cake. Not exactly five-star, but the effort alone gave the whole thing added flavor.

My throat clenched around the third bite of sandwich as a familiar silver BMW turned into the lot and slid into the spot next to mine. I took a long swig of soda, barely getting it down before Victor Itachi's long frame emerged from the cab.

"Hello, Redmond," he said with an oil-slick grin.

"Mister Itachi."

"I want to apologize for the other night," he said. "Let me take you to lunch."

I lifted my sandwich. "I'm covered, thanks."

"I see." His sharp eyes bored into me as I took another bite as if searching for weakness. "I need to drop off my car."

My eyes immediately jerked to the vehicle over his shoulder. "Is there a problem?"

"With your work? No. Just regular maintenance. Oil change, tire rotation."

"Oh. Well, just take your keys up front, and—"

He cut me off by dangling his key fob between us. "I want you to do it."

"Why?"

"Bo says you're the best," he said. "I believe him."

"Anyone can do an oil change."

"I want you."

"Well, I'm on my break, so..."

He didn't say anything, but his eyes hardened to a sharp point that made my blood sizzle.

I hesitated, sucking a bit of bread out of my teeth. "Everything is a power play with you, isn't it?"

His smile lengthened, the key still swinging between us. I released a long breath before snatching it out of his hand.

"I plan to finish my lunch," I said, taking another deliberate bite.

"Of course."

"Come back in an hour."

"Okay." Another flash of pearly teeth. He shifted his weight as if to step away but stopped short. "One more thing." He tucked his hand inside his jacket, plucked out a thin rectangle of plastic, and held it out to me. I flinched away from the thing as if it were venomous.

"I told you, that place wasn't for me," I said, my voice coming out a bit rougher than I'd like.

"Oh, I know," he said with a shrug. "I just wanted you to have this. In case you reconsider. Think of it as an open invitation."

I scowled and turned my eyes back to my sandwich. He released a light, airy laugh and laid the key down on the tailgate.

"We're getting together tonight. I hope to see you there."

His hard-soled shoes clicked across the pavement as he walked away. I focused hard on my sandwich, trying not to think about that piece of plastic poised like a snake to strike me. A key. An invite into his private room. My stomach twisted and my food lodged in my throat.

*There's no way I'm going back there. No fucking way.*

I finished up my lunch, probably taking a little longer than I needed just out of spite. When I went inside, I tossed Victor's fob at Lawrence and went to work on Sean's Prius, the keycard poking me every time I reached into my pocket.

# Chapter 8

F*uck fuck fuck what am I doing?*

I sat behind the wheel of my truck staring up at that big house, grip white-knuckle tight on the wheel and sweat gathering at my temples. All I could think about was the face of the grocer from Black Creek. I didn't know why it scared me like it did. As Victor had said, he was here too. I wasn't the only one in town languishing in the closet. The sight of him should have given me hope, but instead it made me profoundly sad. I didn't want to be here. I wanted to go home, work on my stupid car, and forget the whole thing.

But, Victor Itachi.

I pulled the keycard out of my pocket and flicked the plastic between my fingers. A hot tightness started low in my belly when I thought of what it meant. The thought of making my fantasies real. But I also heard the Colonel's voice in my head. The voice that boomed loud over every mistake I ever made.

*Stupid. Worthless. Pervert. Fag.*

"Fuck you, old man," I grumbled under my breath. I closed my eyes and rested my head against the steering wheel. "Come on, Red. It's just sex, for fuck sake. Just get it out of your system."

I raised my head and kicked the door open before I could change my mind. Gravel crunched under my feet as I marched toward the door, hands jammed in my pockets to hide their shaking. A small, feminine laugh greeted me as I climbed the steps. The woman who kept me company that first day, draped over the arm of a new man.

"Well, look who's back," she said with a smirk, eyes glassy with whatever drug she was on.

I ignored her and pushed on to the door with its little knocker. It opened before I even reached for it, the doorman's big head framed in the crack.

"You a member?" he growled, squinting his beady eyes at me.

"I...um..." My mouth went dry and I nearly dropped the keycard as I lifted it to his eye level. "I was invited."

He screwed up his meaty features as he studied both me and the card. Part of me hoped he wouldn't let me in. That I could go home satisfied with my courage yet unblemished by the debauchery within.

Adrenaline surged anew when he swung the door open and jerked his head, turning my knees to rubber. The house was just as I remembered, the wide foyer, the separate parlors, the table littered with accessories. I staggered toward the parlor on the left, dodging a pair of men as they drifted out in a lusty haze.

*No going back now.*

I spotted him as soon as I crossed the threshold. Victor Itachi enthroned on one end of a long leather couch, the boy, Toby, draped across his lap. His dark gaze drifted over the room's occupants as he dragged his fingers lazily through Toby's hair.

"Redmond." My name fell from his lips like sugar water, his eyes brightening when they stopped on me. Toby's head jerked up, a jealous scowl twisting his youthful features.

"Victor." My voice cracked and my cheeks burned.

"I'm glad you made it." He snapped and Toby sat up, the charm on his collar clinking. His eyes widened and lips parted with a little gasp as Victor lifted out of the sofa like something made of air and drifted toward me. "Would you like to have a seat? Perhaps, a drink?"

"No...I...uhh..." The gears in my head screeched to a halt. I was already hard. Jesus Christ, what was wrong with me?

The corners of his lips ticked upward. "Something more private then." He laid his delicate fingers over the card still clutched in my hand. I released it, embarrassed at the dampness I left behind. "Come with me."

Palms sweating, blood rushing in my ears, I followed Victor Itachi up the stairs and down a narrow hallway lined with doors. We squeezed past all manner of couples in all stages of congress. He stopped just past a butch lesbian, her hand roughly working under her vociferous partner's skirt, and slid his keycard into a lock. The door swung open silently and he slipped inside without even a glance in my direction. I panicked. Passing through that door felt like a page being turned, a decision made with far-reaching and irreversible consequences.

Holding my breath, I stepped through the door. Victor stood before me, his back turned. He slipped his jacket off his narrow shoulders and tossed it on the bed. The bed. God. Just a basic, full-sized bed with a generic tan comforter, but the sight of it made my guts clench. Just a plain old room, but after everything I'd witnessed, even the tissue box on the nightstand seemed lewd.

"Are you okay?" I jumped at the sound of Victor's voice in the relative silence. He'd turned to face me and plucked at the buttons on his collar.

"Huh? Oh...yeah," I answered. My mouth was dry, and I swallowed twice to get my tongue moving again.

"Don't be nervous," he said and took a step toward me. I flinched back, knocking into the slightly ajar door and slamming it closed.

"I'm not nervous."

Victor laughed, a low, sultry laugh, and took another step closer. His cologne filled my head and made me dizzy. Musty and sweet like new leather.

"It's just..."

"Been a while?"

"Yeah."

"How long?" He was so close, now, I could feel his body heat.

"Two...maybe three..."

"Months?"

"Years."

A dark smile stretched across Victor's face and he slid his hands over my hips. I flinched instinctively as his fingertips teased up the hem of my shirt and tickled the bare skin of my lower back. I was taller than him, though not by much, and our hips notched together as if we were made to fit each other.

"Have you ever had a dog?"

I blinked. "A dog?"

"Dogs make wonderful companions. Full of unconditional affection."

"Uh huh..."

"Do you want to be my dog, Redmond?" he breathed into my neck. "Give me your affection, follow my rules, and I'll take good care of you."

"R-rules?" My skin burst into flame as he pushed my shirt up under my armpits and his tongue teased my earlobe. For a moment, I forgot where I was and what he was offering as I imagined his tongue all over me, teasing me, tasting me, my breathing coming in short pants.

"Obedience. Loyalty. Stay. Heel. *Beg.*" He sucked hard at the skin behind my ear, making my back arch and my vision blur. "Give me your trust and I'll give you what you need. Good dogs get treats."

"And bad ones?" Sharp pain cut through the haze as he bit down hard, making me squeal, followed by more licking and sucking. The combination of sensations left me confused, unsteady, and I clutched onto his sleeves to keep from falling. This was nothing like my fantasy. It wasn't romance. It wasn't sweet or tender, but primal and my body screamed for it.

"Do you have a safe word?" he asked. I shivered despite the heat building in my core. I couldn't speak, so I just shook my head. "Now would be a good time to come up with one."

"I—I don't—" His teeth tightened on my earlobe again and panic shot through me. Safe word. A way to tell him to stop. "Brakes!"

"Good boy," he said with a low laugh. "Any hard noes?"

"Uhhm..." I shook my head in an effort to focus, but it was no use.

"That's okay. We'll figure them out as we go."

I groaned as he pulled back long enough to pull my shirt over my head. Shit, this was really happening. His long hair tickled my chest as he sucked at the skin of my collarbone and down my sternum. I tensed when his teeth grazed my nipple, but this time they were gentle, sending ripples of heat straight to my pelvis.

A low whine slipped past the knot in my throat and I arched off the wall toward him, curling my fingers in his hair and pulling him tighter against me. He growled and jerked back, grabbing me by the wrists and slamming them into the wall beside my head.

"Did I say you could touch me?" The same hard but cold tone he'd used in the restaurant and just like then, I couldn't help but respond.

"I'm sorry, I'm sorry," I muttered. Adrenaline once again cut through the fog, lending everything startling clarity. The sting of his nails digging into my wrists, the dangerous sharpness of his eyes, his pretty lips curled into a snarl.

"'I'm sorry, *sir*,'" he corrected, his face so close to mine his breath brushed my lips.

"I'm sorry, sir." The words came out a shuddering gasp. Fear and lust fused in a hot amalgamation inside me and I couldn't breathe.

"Look at you, so needy for your Master." He drew closer once again, his chest against mine, pinning me tight against the wall. "I bet you'd even hump my leg if I let you."

I shuddered and his scowl turned into a mischievous grin. He shifted his hips, thrusting his leg between mine, his thigh pressing against the ever-growing bulge in my jeans.

"Go ahead. Hump it."

Heat splashed my cheeks and I gritted my teeth. No way, no fucking way I was humping his leg like some damn dog, and yet the thought made my cock twitch. The thought of being pinned by him, controlled by him, had my head reeling with a combination of humiliation and need.

I pushed my hips forward. My cock dragged along his thigh, the friction sending a shower of sparks over my skin. He hummed in encouragement as I rolled my hips in a stuttering rhythm. My eyes caught his and a flash of shame made me turn away.

His grip on my wrists tightened. "Look at me, Redmond."

"I can't." My voice came out rough and jittery.

"Why not?"

My whole body quaked. I opened my mouth to answer but all that came out was a groan.

"You want me to stop, just say the word."

I didn't want him to stop and the realization scared me. He scared me. His cold eyes, his firm grip. I probably had twenty pounds on him and yet I was helpless. A slave to the desires he stirred up in me.

He brushed his lips across my cheek, and I whimpered again. "Look at me."

I shook my head and squeezed my eyes shut. Victor growled and brought his knee up into my crotch just hard enough to be uncomfortable.

"Do you want to go back to your boring life? Do you want to wait another three years for someone to touch you? Look. At. Me."

I opened my eyes and reluctantly turned to meet his. I expected anger, disgust, disappointment, but there was only desire. I rolled my hips again and he pushed back, increasing the pressure and friction of every stroke. My long, crushing dry spell meant tension mounted fast and splotches of pink colored his cheeks as I rode him harder, moaning with abandon.

"That's a good boy, Redmond." His lips were just millimeters from mine, and I craned forward, but he was always just out of reach. "You want to come already, don't you?"

*Fuck* yes, I did, but the response came out a string of whimpers as I ground my hips into his. He kissed me hard and then he was gone. My knees gave out, and I fell to the floor, my hips still twitching and thrusting into nothing. I released a mournful cry as my impending orgasm receded, leaving me raw.

"Why..." I gasped, curling into a ball as he loomed over me. He didn't answer. He turned his back on me and crossed the room to an armchair shoved in the corner. He fell into it with a heavy sigh, shifting uncomfortably before yanking his pants open and shoving his hand inside. With a moan of relief, he dragged the flat of his palm over his own erection.

"Come here." Breathless, hand still working over himself, he patted his knee. I pulled myself upright, unbuttoning my own fly with a groan before struggling to my feet. "No," he said sharply. "Hands and knees. And leave your pants."

*You must be fucking kidding me.*

Humiliation coursed through me again, and I felt a tug on my cock as if he had his hand around it. My skin burned white-hot. He tapped his knee again, eyes hardening with impatience. I had two choices: sit here and watch him jack off, my own unreleased orgasm souring in my balls, or do as he said. Shame gave way to desperation as I kicked my way out of my pants and crawled on hands and knees across the floor toward him.

"Good dog," he said with a glassy-eyed grin. "Now, stay."

Blinking, I rocked back on my haunches. His hand continued to work inside his pants, his expression slack and eyes dark.

"W-what is this?" I trembled with need. He'd brought me close, so close, and now he wouldn't even touch me.

"Training."

His hips jerked and his breathing went jagged, his eyes locked with mine. My cock throbbed and my hand drifted toward it.

"I said, *stay!*"

I flinched, jerking my hand away and pressing it flat to the floor. Sweat ran down my back and my breathing came in harsh puffs. Victor's eyes raked over me, leaving a trail of heat behind them. Muscles aching, cock leaking, I'd never felt so exposed.

"Please..." My plea came out a gasp.

"I'll give you what you need when you're ready for it."

His voice slid over me, both threat and assurance. Little by little, the storm inside me quieted, replaced by a low hum like a perfectly tuned engine. My muscles relaxed and I melted into the floor, back bowed, head low.

"Good. That's good, Redmond. Now, come sit on my lap."

I lifted my eyes slowly. My joints felt loose, my bones like putty as I crawled toward him and settled myself on his knee. He grabbed me roughly by the hips and yanked me back into him. Fuck me, his cock was out. His hot flesh pressed against my back.

"You're doing so well," he breathed, lips brushing against the shell of my ear. He curled his fingers around my wrists again, guiding my hands to the arms of the chair and pressing my palms into the fabric. His command unspoken. Stay.

Everything went still. Everything but his hands and his breath on the back of my neck. He slid his palms up my arms and across my chest, dragging his nails over my nipples and making me hiss. I was dizzy with want, wild with it, my muscles aching with the effort of remaining motionless. I was both in my body and out of it, that evil part of me watching in disgust at my perversion, the other wanting desperately to fall apart in his hands.

Victor let his right hand drift lower, triggering a long whine. "Do you want me to touch you?"

"No. Fuck. Yes." I dropped my head back on his shoulder, gasping as he just brushed the base of my cock only to pull away.

"Then, trust me." He sucked a line of kisses along my outstretched neck. "Trust me to take care of you. To give you what you need."

I broke out in goose bumps despite the heat in my core. He traced every part of me, my chest, my back, my thighs, until I quivered all over. Finally, he moved one hand back to my cock, this time wrapping tight around the base, and I released a choked cry.

"Relax, Redmond." He didn't move, simply held me in his grip.

"I can't—" My words cut apart by ragged gasps. "Please, sir. Please. I can't take it."

"You can."

I shook my head, flinging beads of sweat in every direction.

"You can. I've got you. Just let go. Let me take care of you."

His voice wavered, evidence of his own struggle, and he leaked against my back. I closed my eyes and willed myself to relax, allowing my body to mold to his. He hummed his approval, settling his free hand against my hip.

He pushed upward into me, his cock sliding against the cleft of my ass, and my body trembled as if he were inside me. My hole clenched and my dick throbbed. He whispered words of encouragement against my temple with every stroke and a swirl of emotions rose in my chest. Anger, fear, despair. They fell from my eyes and clogged my sinuses.

"Beg," he said, voice strained as his body jerked beneath me.

"Please!" I threw my head back and poured the words directly in his ear. "Please, sir. Please please please."

His hips snapped wildly into mine. Tears burned in my eyes as finally, finally his hand moved over me, wringing from me a string of sloppy, incoherent curses. A hot, wet burst against my back and he shouted the words I begged to hear.

"Come, dog!"

For a moment, I swear I went blind. Deaf and dumb, too, all senses overwhelmed by the heat exploding inside me. Like a bottle coming uncorked, I emptied myself onto the floor in a great gush. My skin twitched as pleasure slid through me, wrapped around me, filled every part of me. The shell I'd built around myself flew apart and as the tension released, my bones turned to Jell-O. Victor released his iron grip on me and, unable to hold myself up, I slid off his lap into a heap on the floor. I couldn't move. Didn't want to move. I wanted to lie there on the floor at his feet until I died.

"Redmond?" I jerked at the touch of his fingers on my cheek. "Time to put the brakes on, okay?" I nodded, groaning as the floor tilted beneath me. He settled down beside me and swept his hand through my sweat-damp hair. "Tell me what you need."

*What I need?* What did I need? As my vision cleared and his face swam into focus, all I could think about was how beautiful he was. How I wanted to bury my face in his long black hair and drown.

\* \* \*

He bathed me. After I'd gathered myself enough to walk, he led me to the steel, claw-foot tub already half full with warm water and dropped me into it. Perched on a wooden stool, his sleeves rolled up to his elbows, he plunged a sponge into the water and worked up a lather. I sat on my rump, knees pulled up to my chest as he scrubbed every part of me. My back, my armpits, even behind my ears.

It embarrassed me at first to be treated so much like a child, but as the ritual went on, it changed. Became comfortable, intimate. I relaxed into his touch, leaning on his arm as he washed my hair.

"How do you feel?" he asked, running his fingers down the line of my spine.

"Safe," I answered with a sigh. "It's weird. I was so scared before."

"You don't need to be scared." He stood, gesturing for me to do the same, and wrapped me up in a big, fluffy towel.

"I don't?"

"No. Trust me, submit to me as a pet does his Master and I will take care of you. I want to take care of you."

He pulled me into a long, slow kiss and wrapped up as I was, I could only give in. I wanted to give in. To all of it. I wanted to drop my insecurities at his feet, to hand over my deepest, most fragile fears and trust him to keep them safe.

"What about Toby?" I asked when we parted. "Is he your pet too?"

He laughed, a clipped, dismissive laugh. "Toby is a Pomeranian. High-maintenance and yippy as hell. He's fun, but only in small doses." He slipped one arm inside the towel and looped it around my waist, sending sparks across my skin. "You are a Great Dane. Noble and strong."

A smile tugged at my lips before settling into something more pensive. "He wears a collar. With your name on it."

He kissed my neck. "Mmmhmmm."

"Will you give me one? I mean, if I'm your dog, now?"

He pulled back a little and a strange emotion flickered across his face. "The collar is a commitment. For both of us. Let's not put the cart ahead of the horse, Redmond."

"But—"

"When you're ready. When *we're* ready."

I nodded and he gave me a peck on the nose before releasing me. "Get dressed."

"Yessir."

I drifted out of the bathroom to gather up my things still piled on the floor by the door. I expected to feel dirty after what we'd just done, but I'd never felt so clean. Like I'd been baptized, all my sins drained away with the bathwater.

"Jesus, it's late," I said, sneaking a peak at my phone as I pulled on my pants. "I've gotta get home."

"Don't tell me you have someone waiting for you," Victor said, pulling down his sleeves and buttoning his cuffs. "I'm jealous."

"My sister." I flinched a little, cursing the fog still clinging to my brain. I was unsure how much of my personal life I was willing to share with a man who treated his lovers like dogs.

Is that what we were, now? Lovers? My cheeks burned and I turned my back. We were practically strangers and yet I'd bared so much of myself to him. He'd reached down inside me and pulled out something ugly I wasn't quite sure I was ready to look at.

"You've done nothing wrong." He appeared behind me, hands on my shoulders, his lips pressed against my ear.

"This is crazy," I said, leaning back into him.

"Maybe, but don't you feel better?"

I did feel better. Before tonight, I was a walking pressure cooker ready to blow and he turned me down to a low simmer. Pleasantly warm without the violent consequences.

"I'll see you again."

I nodded.

"Good. Now, go."

He sent me off with a sharp swat on the butt and I skipped out of the room with a yip, riding a cloud so high, I thought I'd never touch back down.

\* \* \*

The next morning, I woke early. For a long time, I just lay in bed staring at my cracked ceiling. I felt...different. Good, different, like my skin fit a little looser. Every part of me tingled with remembered sensations, bringing a smile to my lips.

Was this what happy felt like? It had been so long, I'd almost forgotten.

The sun pushed its way through my little square window, a reminder the real world beckoned. I rolled out of bed, all my muscles loose as spaghetti noodles, and staggered to the kitchen to start breakfast. A little of my happiness fell away when I spotted the pile of bills on the counter.

The real world sucks.

I slipped the past due electric bill out of the pile and, after a quick glance down the hall to Katie's room, punched the billing information number into my phone. Time to grovel for yet another extension. I was flipping through a list of tried and true excuses when a clipped female voice answered the line.

"I'm calling about a past due balance on my account." I cleared my throat to dislodge the stone in my larynx.

"Account number?"

I read the number off my bill, the pause after filled with a flourish of sharply struck keys. "The thing is...I've been having kind of a hard time and I was just wondering—"

"There's no balance on that account, sir."

I blinked. "Excuse me?"

"Your account has been paid in full." She said the words slowly, each one conveying her irritation.

"There must be some mistake..."

"Redmond Cole, three-two-eight-nine Cedar Street?"

"Yes."

"No mistake," she said. "Says here your lawyer called."

My mouth went dry. "Lawyer?"

"Mister Victor Itachi."

Shit.

"He paid your balance and instructed all future billing to be forwarded to his office."

*I'll take good care of you.*

"Son of a bitch."

"Sir?"

"Nothing. Sorry." A giddy laugh bubbled up from inside me and I had to bite my tongue to keep it down. "Th-thank you...for your...Thank you."

I hung up the phone just as Katie rounded the corner, scratching at her sleep-matted hair and yawning. She yelped as I jumped out of my chair and wrapped my arms around her.

"What the hell? It's six a.m., you psycho!" She shoved me away, but not before I planted a big kiss right on the top of her greasy head. "What's got into you?"

"Nothing," I said, prancing backward into the kitchen. I grabbed the trashcan on my way and swept the pile of mail into it. "Pancakes?"

# Chapter 9

A week passed and I had finally gotten all the spray paint off Sean's car. It just needed a good wax to save the topcoat. Guilt clogged my pores as I worked the creamy compound, making me sweat. I hadn't seen or spoken to Sean since our disastrous fishing trip. Not that I didn't want to. That one night made me realize how badly I needed companionship, a friend who understood what I was going through even if he didn't know I was going through it. Someone to make me feel like less of a freak.

But I was afraid. Afraid of what that friendship meant and the risks of pursuing it. Afraid, maybe, of accepting the part of myself I'd grown so accustomed to hating.

I'd seen Victor Itachi three times.

I ducked my head, working the wax a little harder as my skin heated with the thought of him. After our first session, I'd spent all night scouring the internet researching different types of BDSM, specifically pet play. Images of men and women dressed in leather dog masks and tails dangling from butt plugs filled my screen. I was appalled at first. The idea of subjugating myself to such a degree made my chest hot and my cock swell. Then I remembered that low hum, the quiet that came with giving in and with each session, I slipped into the role a little easier, the line between Master and dog a little thicker. I knew exactly what he expected of me. I didn't have to think or worry.

Obey and your Master will take care of you.

"Hey, Red! Phone call!" Lawrence yelled into the garage, waggling the phone receiver in my direction. "I think it's your sister's school."

I groaned and wiped the wax off my hands. Katie's suspension was almost over and I'd yet to set up a meeting with her teacher. Sounded like they were saving me the trouble.

"This is Red."

"Mister Cole?" A nasal voice made thin by the speaker asked with feigned authority. "This is Sandra Knight, secretary at Black Creek High School. Is this Kaitlyn Cole's father?"

"Brother."

"Excuse me?"

"Katie's my sister."

"Oh." A pause. "Are you her *legal* guardian?"

"She lives with me," I said, prickling with irritation. "I've raised her since she was thirteen. If you have a problem, you talk to me. Is there a problem, Miss Knight?"

"I see." I could practically see her clutching her pearls. "Well, as I'm sure you know, Mister Cole, your sister has had some... trouble in the classroom."

"Yes, I'm aware," I said, rolling my eyes.

"The principal thinks it's a good idea for all of us to have a sit down, you, Kaitlyn, and her teacher, before her return to class on Monday. To ensure everyone knows what's expected of her."

A defensive ire boiled in my belly and I gritted my teeth against it. My eyes dropped to a day-old newspaper tossed on the countertop and I scanned the headlines as a distraction. The local section. Sports teams, farmer's markets, obituaries.

*Patricia Delaney, Heiress of Delaney Lumber, Dead at 72*

"Fuck."

"Excuse me?"

"S-sorry, that wasn't—" My mouth went dry and I couldn't catch my breath. Patricia Delaney. Sean's mother.

"How is tomorrow afternoon for you?" she asked. "Four o'clock."

"Yeah, whatever. That's fine," I said, pulling the newspaper toward me. She was still talking when I dropped the receiver into the cradle. Phrases jumped off the page and sank into my skin. *Died peacefully at home. Survived by a cousin and two brothers.* No mention of her son. *Services to be held tomorrow at 11:00 a.m.*

Yesterday's paper. I glanced at my watch. If I left now, I could just make it.

I didn't know how to explain it to my coworkers, so I didn't. I grabbed my keys out of my locker and jumped in my truck. I raced as fast as I dared in the old clunker to the only cemetery in town. Monuments grew from the ground like trees, a forest of granite, and I weaved my truck along the winding path until I spotted the knot of mourners gathered around a fresh plot. I spotted Sean standing apart from the group, head bowed, alone.

I parked the truck at the end of a long line of black cars. I watched from the cab as the pastor took his place behind a podium, his Bible open across the top, ready to launch into all the same platitudes meant to offer comfort to the living. But I knew better. I knew the anger, the loss, the gaping hole that could never be filled. No words, no matter how profound, could change that.

With my heart aching, I swung the door open and got out. Sean's eyes lifted at the sound of the creaking door and widened in surprise. I offered him a sad smile, and though his chin wobbled, the corners of his mouth lifted in acknowledgment. I couldn't join them, dressed in my greasy coveralls, but this was enough. Enough to show him he wasn't alone.

Services ended and the crowd dispersed, some to their cars,

others gathering in pods to gossip and make plans for the day. Sean lingered a moment at the graveside, hands shoved in his pockets, before taking a deep breath and drifting toward me.

"Hey," he said.

"Hey." I glanced over his shoulder at the receding tide of mourners. "Big turnout."

"Yeah, it's the social event of the season," he said bitterly. He studied me with red-rimmed eyes. "What are you doing here?"

"I saw in the paper. About your mom," I said, shuffling my feet. "Thought you might need a friend."

"Are we friends, Red?"

"I'd like to be." I ducked my head as heat crawled up my neck. "Look, I'm sorry about the other day. That was really shitty."

"It's okay. I'm used to it."

"It's not okay," I said. "I thought I was better. I want to be better."

"Well...this is a good start." He smiled a little, his expression softening. He took a deep, shaky breath before leaning on the truck next to me. "God, I hate these people."

"The cream of society," I said with a dry laugh. "You wanna get out of here?"

He arched an eyebrow in my direction. "You sure? Someone might see you leave with me."

I scanned the crowd of dark-clad mourners, all their heads huddled together and noses in their handkerchiefs. They paid no mind to the son of the deceased. Just like that article in the paper, they were pretending Sean didn't exist.

"I'll risk it."

\* \* \*

After a quick stop for a case of beer, we ended up at Sean's secret fishing hole. Without poles or tackle, there was little more to do than stare out over the water, rippling and golden under the midday sun. Sean's grief cast a dark shadow over him despite the brightness, and I could tell by his lost expression he was still there at his mother's graveside, counting his regrets.

"My mom died when I was ten."

Sean's eyes jerked to me, his eyebrows lifting in sympathy. "Jesus. I'm sorry."

"Car accident." I took a long pull off my beer bottle. "I don't remember much. I was so young, when they told me she was dead, I'm not sure I really understood what it meant. All I remember is feeling like someone had taken an ice cream scoop and carved out some part of me I didn't even know was there until it was gone."

Sean sniffled and wiped the back of his hand across his nose. "Does it still feel like that?" he asked, his eyes pinched.

"No...and yes." I scratched at my unkept hair as I struggled to articulate the feeling. "I mean, it's not as raw as it was, but it's still there. Maybe I've just gotten used to missing her."

"So, your sister..."

"My father remarried when I was about fourteen. Then, Katie."

He nodded, rolling the beer bottle between his hands, his eyes going distant again. "My mom...she was always my champion, ya know? Growing up, I was the moon and stars." His eyes shimmered and a smile pulled at his lips. "Even after...she didn't care what I was. Sending me away, that was all my dad. She called me almost every day I was in boarding school, even if it was only for a few minutes, just to make sure I was okay. He may not have wanted me, but I was still *her* son, her moon and stars."

His expression crumpled and he hid his face behind his hand, his back shivering with his ragged breaths.

"I'm really alone, now, aren't I?"

I blinked, swallowing a sticky ball of emotion, and laid my hand on his back.

"No, you're not."

# Chapter 10

Katie and I sat next to each other in hard, plastic chairs in a deserted classroom papered with motivational posters. "Reach for the stars." "Anything is possible." My nose itched with the smell of antiseptic and pencil shavings, and my head crowded with the sour memories of a misspent youth. Katie had her arms crossed tight over her chest, her expression hard. The irritation of listening to adults talk about you as if you weren't there, as if your opinion didn't matter. I reached over and squeezed her shoulder.

"I'm on your side, kiddo," I said with a wink. Her posture loosened a notch and the corner of her mouth ticked up.

The door swung open, admitting a pair of middle-aged ladies in outdated power suits and too much perfume. They planted themselves on the other side of a Formica table. The one opposite me, obviously the alpha of the pair, laid a manila folder marked "Kaitlyn Cole" on the table in front of her. She folded her manicured hands on top of it.

"Mister Cole," she said, flashing a tight smile. "My name is Miss Jansky. I'm the principal here at Black Creek High." She gestured to the petite lady next to her, red nails flashing. "And this is Kaitlyn's chemistry teacher, Mrs. Benjamin."

Mrs. Benjamin shifted in her seat before giving me a curt nod, the bun at the back of her head bouncing. Her eyes shifted between Katie and me, her hands clutched in her lap.

"Mister Cole, as you know, there have been some concerns raised about Kaitlyn's behavior." She opened the file in front of her and flicked through the pages. "She's disruptive, rude, challenges the authority of her teachers—"

"My understanding is her teacher was giving out wrong information."

Mrs. Benjamin blinked, her cheeks going pink.

"That is not the issue here, Mister Cole."

"Isn't it?" I said, sitting straighter in my chair.

"There is a right and wrong way—"

"I agree," I said, "and we've had a discussion about that." I glanced over at Katie and she lowered her eyes, her bottom lip poking out. "I'm only suggesting that the punishment may have been a bit extreme. Perhaps stemming from Mrs. Benjamin's embarrassment."

The teacher flinched and her blush deepened.

"Mister Cole, your sister is a problem."

"The *problem* is your inability to challenge her," I said, slapping my hand on the table. "She's a smart girl and she's bored. Maybe instead of feeling threatened—"

"Mister Cole." The principal snapped the folder shut, her expression turning to granite. "Perhaps we should have a word alone."

She shot a pointed look to the teacher at her side who hurriedly gathered herself and scooted out of the door. Jaw clenched, I handed Katie my keys and told her to wait at the truck. She popped out of her seat, chin high.

"Where are your parents, Mister Cole?" the principal asked after a dense silence.

"Excuse me?"

"Raising a teenager can be...trying. Especially one as willful as your sister."

Steam boiled beneath my skin. "What are you implying?"

"A child needs her parents."

"A child needs a home where she feels safe and loved," I said. "The two are not always the same."

"She needs structure. Discipline."

"You saying I can't give her that?"

"How many hours a week do you work, Mister Cole?"

"Oh, fuck you," I said, my chair squealing as I pushed back from the table.

"How many hours does she spend alone, unsupervised?"

"Do you have this conversation with single mothers?"

"This is not about gender politics, Mister Cole. It's about what's best for Kaitlyn."

"We're done." I pushed away from the table so hard, her papers went skidding across the surface.

"I've been looking over her file, Mister Cole." Her tone made my heart seize. I stopped just short of the door and pivoted on my heel. Her eyes were hard, her mouth set in a grim line. "You signed her high school enrollment documents, but everything before that was signed by a Colonel Cecil Redmond Cole. Navy Retired."

My skin went cold. "Your point?"

"It likely fell through the cracks due to the similarities in your name..."

I leaned forward, clenching my fists. "Are you threatening me?"

"No, of course not." Her eyes softened and she let out a breath. "Just expressing concern. If this behavior continues and your custody is called into question—"

"Fuck you." I marched back toward her and pressed my clenched fists against the tabletop. "You want to know about *Colonel* Cecil Redmond Cole's discipline?"

She leaned back in her chair. "Mister Cole—"

"Do you want to hear about a nine-year-old boy forced to stand at attention for hours while his father sat in an armchair, a riding crop across his knees, ready to whip him if his posture faltered? How he pissed down his leg and nearly collapsed from exhaustion before he let him go, all because he put his elbows on the table at dinner? Tell me again how a child needs her parents."

Ms. Jansky's shoulders slumped and her eyes softened. She opened her mouth to speak, but I stomped out of the room and slammed the door behind me. Hot with rage, cold with panic, I flung myself down the hall and through the big double doors. I stopped on the front steps, sun blinding me, heart pounding in my ears.

"That. Was. Awesome!" Katie's voice broke through the fog. She stood next to my old truck, eyes bright, bouncing on the balls of her feet. "Best big brother ever!"

"Get in the truck," I said in a hoarse voice.

Her expression dropped. "What happened?"

"Just get in the truck, Katie."

"Red—"

"Get in the fucking truck! Why can't you just do as you're told?"

She pressed her back against the cab, eyes wide and tearful. Regret slammed through me, but the anger burned hotter.

"I'm trying, Kaitlyn, I really am, but you make it so fucking hard." I paced the lot in front of her, breath coming in ragged gasps.

"What are you saying, Redmond?" she asked, lips trembling.

"I need you to stop getting into trouble. Stop skipping class. Stop giving your teacher lip, even if she deserves it. I am killing myself to keep this family together—"

"Red—"

"I need you to be on *my* side."

"Okay. I'm sorry." She threw her arms around me, burying her head in my chest as tears cut down her cheeks. I held onto her so tight, it must have hurt, but she didn't say a word.

\* \* \*

When we got home, she went straight to her room and closed the door. The panic leaked out of me, leaving only a cold dread that made my palms sweat and my headache. I dropped down on the sofa, exhausted and raw. The principal's words rattled around in my head like a bad omen.

*Are you her legal guardian?*

Tears pricked at the back of my eyes and I pressed the heels of my hands against them so hard I saw stars. I thought of every time she drove me crazy, every time I resented having her with me. Maybe her principal was right. Maybe she would be better off with the Colonel's harsh brand of discipline than none at all.

A chorus of barking dogs jarred me out of my daze. My phone. I knew who it was, knew what the text message would say without even looking.

*Heel.*

Like flicking a switch, the turmoil inside me quieted. No more need to be afraid. My Master called.

I took a long breath before pulling myself up and walking to the closed door of my sister's room. I gave it a quick one-two-three tap with my knuckles. It swung inward a little. It wasn't even latched. "Katie?" No answer. Another quick tap before easing it open.

Katie lay on her side, curled into a fetal position, tapping through screens on her phone with one hand. She didn't look up when I sat on the edge of her bed.

"I'm going out for a little while," I said, laying a hand on her shoulder. "You gonna be okay?"

"Sure. Whatever," she said in monotone, gaze never leaving her phone. Her green eyes were glassy and rimmed in red.

"Okay." I squeezed her shoulder, hesitating a moment before standing up.

"Maybe I should go home," she said just as my hand touched the doorknob.

My heart seized. "This is your home."

"To Mom and Dad's, I mean." Her eyes were still on her phone, but the tapping stopped.

"Why do you think that?"

She shrugged, biting her lip to keep it from trembling. I sat back down on her bed.

"Is that what you want?"

Her eyes pinched and a stubborn drop fell down her nose. "No. Is it what you want?"

"No, of course not." I had hardly the air to form the words. She tucked the phone against her chest and pushed her face into the pillow. I ran my fingers through her hair and had a sudden flash of her thirteen-year-old face, tear-streaked, as she stood on my front porch with nothing but a backpack.

"Do you remember when you first came here?"

She turned her face just enough to look at me through the corner of one eye and nod.

"You were so small and so scared. You hardly knew me, but you looked at me like I was a superhero." I swallowed hard as the memory of that night rose to choke me. "You'd gotten into a fight with the Colonel—"

"He's an asshole—" I cut her off with a stern look and she pushed her nose back into the pillow with a weak, "Sorry."

"When I called to let them know you were okay, he..." My heart rate kicked up a tick at the memory of his sharp, military clip. Even over the phone, he scared me.

.  .  .

"What do you want, boy?" The air changed when he answered, as if his malicious aura had crawled up the line.

"Nothing, sir. I just..." Jesus, Red, get it together. You're not fifteen anymore. "Just wanted to let you know Katie was here."

He huffed but didn't respond. I'd sent Katie to the bathroom to wash up and now she peered at me from around the corner, her big, watery eyes and a shock of red hair the only thing visible from the doorway.

"I think she should stay here for a while."

"Excuse me?"

My mouth went dry and I clenched my fists. "I think she needs a break—"

"You think you're a better father than me, boy?"

"No, sir. I—"

"Fine. You two want to play house, go ahead. Don't you dare come to me for help."

"I don't want anything from you," I snapped. The line went silent for a long time and sweat broke out on my forehead. In my youth, such insolence would see me sleeping outside in the rain with only, if he were feeling charitable, the clothes on my back.

"You have one chance," he said, a threat implicit in his tone. "Do not disappoint me."

Katie's hand wrapped around mine and only then did I realize I was shaking. "I didn't know what to do. I didn't know anything about taking care of a kid. I could barely take care of myself. But I couldn't send you back there."

I closed my eyes and took a deep, shuddering breath as I struggled to shake off the memory. It crawled over my skin like spiders, making my hair stand up and my palms sweat. Nothing had changed. He still scared me. Worse, because I was scared for her.

"I still don't know what I'm doing, ya know?" My voice cracked around the admission and I squeezed her hand between mine. "So, I need you to help me out. We've gotta be a team, okay? Have each other's backs no matter what."

When I opened my eyes, I found hers, big and bright, looking back at me. Lips pursed, brows furrowed, she threw her arms around my neck and buried her head in my chest. My throat tightened as her back shook with ragged sobs.

"Hey, look at me," I said, giving her shoulders a squeeze. She took a shaky breath before looking up, her eyes red and swollen, and I wiped the tears away with my thumb. "I will always want you here. Unless you trash my kitchen again. Then you're out."

"That's not funny." She laughed and scrubbed at her face, though the tears kept falling.

"I know. Worst brother ever, right?"

"Na, you're okay." She sniffled and wrapped her hand in mine. Even now, three years later, all I saw was that scared but hopeful little girl who needed me.

"I'm sorry I yelled at you."

She dropped her eyes and her bottom lip poked out. "S'okay."

"I don't have to go, ya know."

She shook her head. "You can go."

"You sure?"

"Yeah, I'm okay now." She scrubbed the tears from her cheeks and lifted her face, forcing a melodramatic smile.

"Well, that's hideous."

We both laughed and the sound carried our tension away with it. I swept the auburn hair out of her face and kissed her forehead. "Good night, kiddo."

"'Night, brother."

\* \* \*

When I got there, he was already waiting for me. Victor sat on the sofa, finely dressed in his typical tailored suit and sipping a glass of wine, his leash coiled beside him. Like the prince of some exotic, fantastical nation, observing his surroundings but above them, narrow eyes hooded and a slight smile curving his lips.

I waited for him to notice me. Standing in the doorway of the foyer, my worries fell away as I slipped into my role piece by piece. His eyes flicked up to me and the knot in my stomach loosened.

He said nothing, simply tapped his knee with his fingers. I dropped to my hands and knees. Despite all the people watching, I knew no shame as I crawled toward him to sit on my haunches at his feet. He stroked my hair. I lay my head on his thigh.

"Are you all right, Redmond? You seem a little...tense."

I closed my eyes and nuzzled tighter against him. We sat like that until he finished his wine, every sweep of his hand over my scalp relaxing me further. I let go of each of those messy emotions one by one, reaching hard for that quiet place, but guilt held fast. Victor tucked a finger under my chin and tipped my head up, squinting down his nose at me, and I squirmed under his appraisal.

He stood without a word, a click of his tongue my only signal to follow. He led me up the stairs to our room. The same, generic room, but now laced with so much meaning. Skin heating, pulse fluttering, I stripped out of my clothes, left them in a neat pile on the floor—Victor liked neatness—and fell once again to my knees.

He gave my head a pat, an unspoken *Good, boy* that made my dick throb, before sliding out of his jacket and tossing it over the back of a chair. He kicked off his shoes and flopped onto his back on the bed. He picked up a magazine, thumbed through it, even clicked on the TV while I patiently waited for his call.

At least, I tried to be patient. I tried to give in, to calm my whiplash emotions, but something inside me resisted. Maybe even resented. I needed him to take care of me and instead, he ignored me. I had no choice but to play his game. Body thrumming, I crawled to the side of the bed, head lowered in submission. A low whine slipped from my throat and his eyes flicked to me, a grin lifting his lips.

"Well, all right, Redmond, come on up."

He patted the space beside him, and I leaped into it, panting and wiggling like an overexcited terrier. I pushed my nose under his hand, nipping and licking at his fingers. He laughed and boxed me lightly on the nose, but his cheeks darkened, all the little affectations of the dog adding to his arousal.

"Good boy, Redmond," he said, giving me a rough scratch behind the ear. "You want a belly rub?"

I nodded and flopped enthusiastically onto my back, arms and legs cockroached in the air. He lay on his side, head supported in one hand, the other making scratching motions over my chest. He started at the base of my throat, quick little scrapes of his nails making my skin tingle. He worked his way down my sternum, following the thin line of hair down my belly and stopping just short of my navel.

"Oh, you want more?" he asked as I pushed up into his hand and whined. He leaned over me. His long hair brushed my shoulder and I nuzzled into it. Flattening his hand, he ran it up my side, around my ribcage, over the planes of my chest, awakening every nerve ending along the way.

I gasped as his fingernails raked over my nipple. "My, you are a needy dog today," he said, voice going husky as I flicked my tongue over his ear. Another scrape and pinch had me clutching his shirt, dizzy with need. He grasped my wrists and gave them a warning squeeze. "You know the rules."

I let out a low groan and tensed against his grip. He held me, eyes hard and unrelenting, until I gave in and sank back into the bed. The corners of his mouth quirked upward, and he laced his fingers through mine as he brushed my lips with a kiss. A small reward for my compliance.

He shifted his body over me, pinning me to the bed. Normally, I relished this, the power and the complete surrender it required. But the day had left me raw. Impatient. The scrape of his clothing over my oversensitive skin was almost painful, and I jerked at every point of contact. He was hard and pressed his cock against my hip, moving in a way that gave him pleasure but left me completely neglected.

Anger flared inside me. I arched my back and pressed my hips forward. Victor growled and pulled back, pinning me with his knee across my thighs. Snarling and snapping, I thrashed against him in an effort to free myself from his grip.

"What's the matter with you, Redmond? Do you want me to punish you?"

Fear shivered through my muscles and I went very still. Victor's black eyes narrowed as he peered into mine. Neither of us moved and I felt only the tightness of his hands around my wrists, the bruising pressure of his knee in my thigh.

He sat back slowly, eyes hard, mouth twisted into a scowl. He didn't restrain me. He didn't have to. All it took was one word.

"Stay."

I whimpered as his dark eyes raked over me. My chest heaved, every muscle twitching with his absence. Sweat gathered on his brow and he gently massaged the bulge at his crotch.

"What a greedy cur you are."

"Wait, please—"

He slid off the bed and disappeared into the bathroom, followed by the sound of running water and banging drawers. Then, nothing. Silence louder than the noise which preceded it, broken only by my own tortured breathing. Sweat made the pillow beneath my head damp as I clenched and unclenched my fists.

When he emerged again, he was naked, his whole body glowing. His dick jumped at the sight of me, just as he left me, sweating and panting with the effort. He walked to the end of the bed, his gaze heated. I groaned as he wrapped a hand around his own cock and gave himself a slow, deliberate stroke.

Heat gathered in my pelvis as he sped his rhythm, head thrown back, eyes hooded but never leaving mine. He wanted me to watch. Wanted me to see. He didn't need me. My pleasure was conditional. His was guaranteed.

My muscles ceased their quivering and my breathing slowed. I deserved this. To watch him take his pleasure and leave. Every orgasm he ever gave me was a reward I had to earn, a prize I had to win, but this time I'd tried to steal it. My action had shown more than impatience, but a lack of trust.

*I'll give you what you need when you're ready for it.*

His abdomen tensed and with a groan he pulled his hand away. He closed his eyes, shivering as he fought back his orgasm, and my cock twitched in sympathy. When his eyes opened, they were hungry. He released me with a snap. I rolled unsteadily onto all fours and wobbled toward him, whimpering, head lowered. Subspace thrummed in my ears as he laid a hand on the back of my head, gently threading his fingers through my hair.

Tears pricked at the back of my eyes. "I'm sorry."

Without a word, he slid his hand underneath my chin and around my neck. With a sharp yank, he brought me up to my knees.

"Your safe word," he said, voice ragged. "Do you remember it?"

"Y-yessir—"

He squeezed. I clutched at his arms, panic clouding my vision as my airway constricted under the pressure. Not enough to cut it off entirely, but enough to feel the threat. The danger. His free hand caught one of my wrists and twisted my arm behind my back, rendering me immobile, even the slightest resistance making my shoulders burn.

Just as the edges of my vision darkened, he relaxed his hand and I gulped at the air in shuddering breaths. I collapsed against him and he held me tenderly, his heartbeat knocking against mine.

"Safe word?"

I shook my head and his grip tightened again. I jerked backward and my knees buckled, sending me onto my back. My legs straddled Victor's hips and I kicked at the empty air. Fear and arousal battled within me. I stood on the edge of a precipice. That wide, empty, clean space opened up before me. I reached for it, but too much stood in my way. All my failures lined up like soldiers keeping me from what I needed.

My head throbbed and my vision blurred. I deserved this. Not just for my disobedience, but for my inadequacy. As a brother. As a lover. As a dog. Yet, still I fought. Kicked and strained and clawed.

*You deserve this. Let him give it to you.*

Tears fell from my eyes as he loosened his grip again. My chest burned as the cool air hit my lungs. Victor loomed over me, his dark eyes full of disappointment.

"You're better than this, Redmond."

A sob broke loose from somewhere deep inside me. He tried to move away, and I clung to his arm. I wasn't even hard anymore. I needed something else entirely.

Something shifted in Victor's eyes. He perched on his knees on the edge of the bed, my legs hooked around his hips. My heartbeat settled into a fast but regular rhythm as his hand rested once again around my throat.

He squeezed and this time, I didn't fight. I closed my eyes, surrendering completely to him. I saw those soldiers lined up in a row, and I let him knock them down. One by one, the voices telling me I wasn't strong enough, wasn't good enough, disappeared under the sound of a rumbling engine.

A thin sound leaked from his throat and he rocked his hips against me. I saw stars as his cock dragged against mine, the sensation heightened by the lack of oxygen. His grip tightened until I couldn't breathe at all. My thighs trembled as he thrust against me hard and steady as a piston. The precipice loomed and I hurled myself over the edge, succumbing entirely to his will.

With a deep groan and a shudder, his release splashed against my thighs. His grip relaxed and my climax hit like a rocket, blasting off from my hips and out of the top of my head. My whole body arched and spasmed, then went ragdoll limp as it passed through me. He held me gently, placing soft kisses along the line of my collarbone before lowering himself down into the bed. He curled up next to me, whispering words of praise in my ear as I gasped and sobbed.

Just like that, it was quiet again.

\* \* \*

It took me a long time to come back down. I clung to him, twitching with aftershocks and panting as if I'd just run a marathon. He waited patiently, fingers running up and down the line of my spine, and after we had both sufficiently recovered, he led me into the restroom for our customary bath. I lay slouched against the side of the tub, wrung out, exhausted in a way that had little to do with my body. Victor had poured himself a glass of wine which he periodically sipped from, holding it to my lips so I could do the same. He was still naked, perched on his little stool, and there was a domesticity to the scene that moved me despite its true shallowness.

"So, are you going to tell me?" he asked, plucking the wineglass off the floor and lifting it to my lips.

"Tell you what?"

"What you need to be punished for."

I hesitated, sipping the wine more to buy time than any real desire to drink it, before letting my head drop back down on the porcelain.

"No."

"Why not?"

"I don't even want to think about it."

He clicked his tongue. The stool scraped across the floor and I gasped as he swung his leg over the side of the tub and climbed in behind me. He'd never gotten in with me before.

"How many times do I have to tell you not to be afraid?" He wrapped his arms around me and rested his chin on my shoulder. His hair spilled over my chest and I let the ends wrap around my fingers in the water. "How can I take care of you if you don't tell me what you need?"

Tears leaped to my eyes as my earlier panic returned to the raw surface. "It's my sister." The words burst out of me before I could stop them. "They're threatening to take her away from me."

"Who?"

"Fucking Principal Jansky with her perfect nails and her fake tits."

Victor's arms tightened around me. "Easy, Redmond. Why would they want to take her away?"

"She...gets into trouble at school. Cuts class, things like that. They're blaming me, like I'm not giving her enough discipline or something."

"And you think they're right."

"Maybe. I work all the time. Can barely keep the lights on and food on the table. I just want to do right by her, to keep her safe. But I'm a failure."

"You're not a failure."

"That fucking school," I said, ignoring him. "She's smart, you know? Real smart. Way smarter than me. She's not getting what she needs there."

"What about a private school?"

"Nearest one worth a damn is in Longview and I can't afford the tuition. If the Colonel finds out—" I clung to Victor's arms as fat tears rolled down my nose. "He'll take her just to punish me. She can't go back there. He'll chew her up. Ruin her. Fuck, what am I going to do?"

He rocked me as everything I'd held back came spilling out of me. He cooed words of comfort in my ear, laying soft kisses on the back of my neck until the fit passed. Once I'd calmed, he stood up out of the bath, handing me the wineglass as he exited.

"Drink that," he said. "Take your time. Come out when you're ready."

He wrapped a towel around his waist, leaving a second within reaching distance of the tub, and left me alone. I pressed the cool glass to my forehead, more than a little embarrassed, but otherwise calmer, as if I'd reached some sort of catharsis. All my fears of inadequacy had been choking me as sure as his hand around my throat. He'd seen that fear in me and responded. Given me what I needed when I didn't know how to ask.

I drained the glass, the wine warming me all the way down to my toes and reached for the towel. When I left the bathroom, Victor was on the phone. He'd partially dressed, his belt buckle jangling around his waist and his shirt hanging open. He waved me over when he spotted me.

"They have some questions for you," he said, shoving the phone against my ear without explanation.

"Mister Cole?" a thin male voice said from the other end of the line.

"Yes? I'm sorry, who is this?"

"This is Daniel Johnson in the registrar's office of Oak Forest Charter School. I just have a few questions regarding your sister's enrollment."

"My sister's..." I shot a look at Victor who focused intently on his buttons. "Is this a joke?"

"No, sir," he said, a little befuddled. "Mister Itachi contacted us regarding her situation at her current school and her aptitude—"

"I'm sorry," I said, "but I can't enroll her in your school. I appreciate the opportunity, but I can't afford—"

"Tuition is covered in full by Mister Itachi, sir."

My jaw dropped. Victor's eyes lifted from his buttons long enough to give me a wink, one corner of his mouth lifting in a sly smile.

"Son of a bitch."

The registrar rattled off a series of questions—full legal name, date of birth, social security number—and directed me to a website where I could download all the necessary forms required upon her first day. Monday. Jesus Christ. My head reeled.

The whole thing took about ten minutes. By the time I was done, Victor had fully dressed and pulled his hair back into a neat ponytail. I crossed the room and practically leaped into his arms. I pulled him into a deep kiss.

"You're welcome," he said with a laugh.

"How can I repay you for this?" I asked. "I'll do anything you want. Blowjobs every day until she graduates. I don't care. I'll do it."

"Blowjobs, while highly encouraged, are not required. I told you. I want to take care of you. You just have to trust me."

"I do trust you." I kissed him again, so relieved I could have melted into the floor. I may have even loved him in that moment and my heart rattled with it.

"A car will be at the house to pick her up at seven, at the school at four to bring her home. If she chooses to do any extracurricular activities, just work out the schedule with the driver."

"Jesus, you've thought of everything."

"Now, get dressed. You should get home and tell her the news."

"Yessir."

# Chapter 11

A car showed up Monday morning just as promised. When I told Katie about our new arrangement, she simply scrunched her face up and shook her head in disbelief, the reality not really taking hold until a black car appeared in the driveway. Her jaw dropped when she saw it.

"Really?"

I laughed. "Really. Now, go or you'll be late on your first day."

She squealed and threw her arms around my neck before bounding out of the door. I'd never seen her so excited to go to school before, never seen her so excited about anything, and it unwound something inside me that had been tight for too long. I finished getting ready for work in a haze, feeling maybe for the first time like I'd done something truly right for her.

"Your boss gouged me." Sean frowned down at his receipt as I pulled his car out of the garage.

"I know. I'm sorry."

He blew out a breath before running his hand over the hood, now devoid of obscenity. His relief was palpable despite the financial cost. A few days had passed since his mother's funeral and only a little of the rawness remained, making the fine lines around his eyes cut a little deeper.

"Hey, what are you doing tonight?" he asked.

"Why?"

"I've got a project going at the house. I think I may have bitten off more than I can chew. Think you could give me a hand?"

"Using me again?"

"Yep. For your muscles, this time," he said, poking me in the chest. "I'll make you dinner."

"I can't. It's my sister's first day at a new school. I wanted to take her out to celebrate."

"So, bring her along. I'll make something fancy."

I sucked in a breath and his expression darkened.

"Right. Never mind."

"It's not that," I said as he shoved past me and into the driver's seat of the Prius. His eyes flicked up at me, full of hurt and disappointment, as he reached for the door. I grabbed it before he could pull it closed. "Sean—"

"Please, let go of the door, Red."

"It's not what you're thinking." A cold finger of panic slid up my spine. "We've...had a rough time lately and I want to spend some time just me and her. That's all."

His expression softened a bit, but he still wouldn't look at me.

"If it can wait until tomorrow, I'm yours. Muscles and all."

The corner of his mouth twitched upward. "Isn't that a thought." He released a long breath, drumming his fingers on the door handle. "Fine. Tomorrow."

"Good," I said, relief flooding through me.

"Don't blow me off."

"I won't."

"Can I go now?" he said, giving the door a tug.

"Yeah," I said with a nervous laugh. I released the door and scratched the back of my neck. He gave a little wave before pulling it shut and rolling out of the lot. Tomorrow. A nervous flutter started in my stomach. If I could just manage not to step in it for one day.

\* \* \*

"Who is Victor Itachi?"

Katie stood in the middle of the living room, arms crossed over her chest and an unfamiliar backpack on the floor at her feet. I hadn't gotten two steps in the door and her question nearly knocked me backward.

"Excuse me?"

"Victor Itachi." She stomped toward me, her face scrunched up and her fists in tight balls at her side. "When I got in the car, there was a bag there full of new supplies. The driver said it was a gift from Mister Itachi. That he worked for Mister Itachi. That my school—"

"Katie, slow down." I grabbed her by her shoulders before she could mow me over.

"Who is he? Why is he doing this? Did you do something, Red?"

"What are you talking about, 'something?'" I pushed her back a step so I could at least get out of the doorway.

"Is he like a mob boss? Is someone going to show up with a mysterious package you have to run over the border or something?"

"Now, you're being ridiculous." I tried to keep my voice light, but my mouth had gone dry.

"Who is he, Red?"

Her cheeks were red and her eyes shone with worry. I swallowed hard, pushing past her into the living room and avoiding her eyes.

"Remember that guy who took me to dinner? The one whose car I fixed?"

"Yeah."

"Well, he and I have been friendly since then—" Understatement. "—and I told him about you and your trouble at school."

"Oh, great," she said, rolling her eyes.

"He offered to help us and I accepted."

"What's the catch?"

"What do you mean, 'catch?' There is no catch."

"There's always a catch, Red. People don't spend thousands of dollars to put someone's kid through school because they fixed their taillight."

"No catch," I said, squeezing her hand. "Promise." She studied me closely before releasing a breath and returning the squeeze. "How was it?"

"Awesome," she said, smiling wide. "Really awesome. The teachers there are brilliant, and they care—really care—about what they're teaching. I think I learned more in one day than I have all year at Black Creek High."

My chest warmed as I listened to her rattle on about the facilities, the other students, her face flushed with excitement and eyes shining. She needed this; we both did. We were going to be okay.

Because of him.

"I think we should celebrate," I said. "Let's go out. Anywhere you want."

She sucked in a breath through her teeth and cringed. "I can't. I have homework."

"You're blowing me off for homework?" I held the back of my hand up to her forehead. "Who are you and what have you done with my sister?"

She laughed and slapped my hand away. "I'm sorry, Red."

"It's okay," I said, but I couldn't hide my disappointment. "I could get a couple of pizzas..."

"That sounds great," she said, beaming.

We spent the next half hour on the couch together while we waited for the pizza. She told me all about the people she met and the things she learned, talking so much and so fast she had to stop periodically to catch her breath. There was a boy in one of her classes, the mention of whom made her blush, and I pined once again for the little girl I'd missed. She'd be grown before long and starting her own life. Soon, she wouldn't need her big brother anymore and the thought made my throat tight.

The pizza arrived and we had one slice together before she disappeared into her bedroom with a second. I relaxed into the couch with a beer, my chest warm. This was the way her life was supposed to be. No tension, no fighting over her behavior and the unfair treatment of her teachers. Just the pure joy of learning something new. For so long, I'd felt like that guy from the Greek myth pushing his rock uphill and never getting anywhere. It might not fix everything, but it was progress and for the first time, the top of the mountain didn't seem so out of reach.

I wanted to share this with somebody. I pulled out my phone and scrolled through my contact list. I thought about calling her mom, letting her know how well she was doing, but just the thought of her indifference soured my good mood. With a small amount of guilt, I flicked past her name only to find my thumb hesitating over another.

Sean Delaney.

My chest buzzed like a beehive. I didn't know why I was so nervous. It was natural, wasn't it, to want to share your achievements with your friends. But his disappointed expression haunted me. Were we friends? Could we ever really be friends with the secrets I was keeping from him?

Before I could talk myself out of it, I clicked on the text message icon and started typing.

*Hey. My sister stood me up. Still need help?*

I balanced the phone on my knee and held my breath. What if he didn't answer? What if I'd already blown it?

My phone chimed, and I jerked so hard I nearly threw it across the room.

*Sure! Bring a set of work gloves and a shovel. We're gonna get dirty ;P*

My held breath released in an explosive laugh. That beehive still buzzing, I popped up off the couch and changed into a pair of torn jeans and a grease-stained T-shirt. I tapped on Katie's door to let her know I was going out, threw a shovel and gloves into the back of my truck, and hit the road.

I pulled into Sean's driveway about twenty minutes later. The backyard floodlights were on, illuminating the place like it was daytime. I grabbed the shovel out of the truck bed and circled around to the back of the house. A line of low hedges flanking an ivy-covered trellis separated the backyard from the front. I passed through the trellis and into the biggest, greenest lawn I'd ever seen. The house was situated on a hillside, and its elevated position gave it a grand, sweeping view of the town. From here, it was almost beautiful, blanketed in velvet nightfall, streetlights twinkling like diamonds at the bottom of a dark sea.

"Red!" Sean waved enthusiastically from the far end of the yard. He looked small against the backdrop, his backward-turned ball cap and flushed cheeks lending his face a boyish quality. His jeans were already streaked with black dirt and a shovel lay at his feet next to a ragged hole.

"Did you call me here to help you bury a body? Because I'm not sure we're that good of friends."

Sean laughed and slapped me on the shoulder. "I know. It's a mess, isn't it?" he said, hands on his hips as he surveyed the wreck-age. A pile of red brick lay half tumbled over a few feet away along with rolls of black plastic sheeting. "You know, the whole time I grew up here, I always wanted a fire pit. Somewhere to hang out and make s'mores. Regular kid stuff. But my parents..." His expression wavered, but he quickly pulled it back together. "Anyway, the place is mine now, so I thought, how hard could it be?"

I leaned on my shovel and peered down at the hack job he'd made of the lawn. He mimicked my posture, standing so close our shoulders touched, setting those bees in my chest to whining.

"I think you've been in the city too long," I teased.

"Is it salvageable?"

I released an exaggerated breath and bit back a smile as his brows pulled together and lips pursed in concern. His boyhood dream rested in my hands. I puffed out my chest, pulled my gloves out of my back pocket, and shoved my hands inside them as if they were a knight's gauntlets.

"Only one way to find out."

We spent the next four hours removing and relocating great mounds of earth until we made a circular pit about four feet in diameter. Sean spent most of that time on his hands and knees, nose pressed to the indicator of a level and directing me where to dig. Once the bottom and the rim were level, we paved the whole thing with brick laid in concentric circles, the gaps filled with Quikrete. We finished it off with a store-bought grate over the top and, while it wasn't perfect, it certainly wasn't bad for a night's work.

"God, I don't think I've ever been so tired in my life." Sean lay on his back in the grass, cap lying beside him and arm thrown over his eyes. Even though it was about a million degrees out and the Quikrete hadn't properly set, I couldn't convince him not to light a fire in the new pit. His skin glowed in the orange light. He'd long ditched his shirt and the shadows clung to the lines of his chest and slid over the plane of his stomach.

"That's because you haven't done a real day's work in your life," I said around the neck of a beer bottle.

"You know, normally I'd be offended, but I think you may be

right." He laughed and propped himself up on his elbows. Despite his exhaustion, his eyes were alight with pride as he examined at the work he'd done, and he couldn't stop smiling. "I couldn't have done it without you though."

My neck heated and I pulled at my earlobe, eyes on the shadows dancing around my feet. "It's no big deal. I was wired, anyway. And I like this sort of work."

"Oh, I almost forgot," he said, reaching for a beer out of the bucket perched between us. "How was your sister's first day at school?"

"Good. Kind of amazing, actually." Now, I couldn't stop smiling. "I've never seen a kid so excited about homework."

"Where is she going, now?"

"Oak Forest Charter School."

He whistled. "It's hard to get in there. And expensive. How'd you manage it?"

"I manage," I said with faux indignation. "Just because I'm not heir to a lumber fortune doesn't mean I'm impoverished, ya know."

"First of all, I'm not heir to anything. My father saw to that," he said, jabbing a finger in the air. "And that's not what I meant. I just—"

"Relax, I know it's not." I picked at the label on my bottle. "We...had help."

"Oh. I see." He took a long pull off his beer and eyed me shrewdly. "You got a sugar momma, Red?"

I coughed violently as my drink nearly came out my nose. "Jesus Christ, Sean."

"Hey, I don't judge," he said, laughing and holding up his hands. "A man has needs. So, who is she? An old widow who inherited a fortune? The wife of a rich oil man who hates her husband, but just can't get enough of the hunk who rotates her tires?"

I threw a chunk of sod at him and he rolled out of its path, laughing like a hyena. "There's no sugar momma, all right." I wrinkled my nose. "And I'm not a hunk."

"You kind of are, actually." He shrugged as I arched an eyebrow in his direction. "So, sue me. I noticed."

The heat on my neck spread to my whole face and I prayed he couldn't see it in the dark. The beehive turned into a full-on hornets' nest. He noticed? What did that mean? That he found me attractive? If I was honest with myself, I would admit I'd noticed him too. The moment he peeled off his sweaty shirt was the best part of my day. But I'd shoved it down deep, down into the same place I put all the other inappropriate emotions I couldn't act on.

But what if I did?

I nearly jumped out of my skin when my phone lit up with that chorus of barking dogs. Sean rolled on the grass laughing as I fumbled in my pockets, kicking and swearing until I managed to rip it out and silence the ringtone. Victor. Shit.

"Speak of the devil?" Sean asked, wiggling his eyebrows.

"It's nobody." Nobody? Fuck. I swiped across my phone until I reached his message, not that I needed to read it.

*Heel.*

I glanced at the time. Nearly midnight. He'd never called so late before. With a knot in my stomach, I tapped out a quick response.

*Can't. Busy.*

"If you need to go…"

"I don't." I flinched as it went off again.

"You know, some girls might find that ringtone offensive."

I rolled my eyes and checked the message.

*Now.*

A sliver of fear slid up my spine. *Do I dare say no?*

"Seriously, it's fine," he said, giving me a friendly punch in the arm.

"Really?"

"Yeah. At least one of us is getting laid."

I groaned and pushed myself to my feet. Normally, a call from Victor would leave me electrified with desire, but my muscles were heavy and sore. I wanted to stay here, curled up on the grass in front of a fire that was too hot.

But my Master called.

# Chapter 12

I t took nearly an hour for me to get showered and changed, and drive to the house. Victor waited in the parlor with a glass of wine as always, only this time Toby the Pomeranian lay draped over his lap.

I stopped short at the sight of them, confusion and jealousy running in hot and cold spurts through my veins. My chest tightened as Victor ran his fingers lazily through his hair and the boy nuzzled deeper into his thigh. He didn't even look up when I made a halting path across the room and knelt at his side.

"Where have you been, Redmond?" His voice was cold, eyes still fixed on the boy in his lap. Toby smirked and watched me closely through a cloud of dark lashes.

"I'm sorry, sir." My mouth went dry, making the words brittle and cracked. "I was...working outside. I had to—"

I gasped as he grabbed me by my shirt front and yanked so hard I nearly bit my tongue. "Who is your Master?"

"You are, sir."

"And don't I take good care of you?"

"Yes, sir."

He wrapped his hand around my neck, squeezing just hard

enough to make me dizzy. His nose bumped against mine, his eyes razor sharp. "That's right. I take care of you, pamper you, give you what you need. I don't ask for much in return. Only obedience. So, there is no *Can't. Busy.* When I say heel, you fucking heel. Got it?"

"Yes, sir." He released me and I hunched over, gasping and coughing. Eyes swung in our direction and their judgement burned into my skin, but none so hot as Toby's amused giggle.

"What am I going to do with you?" Victor said as if to himself. Toby raised his body up to nuzzle Victor's neck, sliding his hand up his thigh. The tag on his collar caught the dim light in silver flashes.

"You could play with me," he whispered into his ear. "I'm a good dog, aren't I?"

"Yes, you are." The words came out a sigh and Victor ran a finger along the boy's jaw. An icy lump formed in my gut as Victor clipped his leash into Toby's collar. Victor stood up and Toby bounced merrily around him. I thought he'd brought me out here just to reject me until he reached down and grabbed me by the scruff of my neck and dragged me behind him all the way up to his room.

It was strange having someone else in here with us. I took my usual place just inside the door, only this time Toby fidgeted beside me, stripping out of his clothes in a flurry of frantic energy. I hesitated, watching Victor for some clue as to how to proceed, but he didn't look at me. He kicked off his shoes and flopped down on the bed as if I wasn't there, as if this wasn't at all different from our usual game.

Slowly, stiffly, I took off my clothes, glancing over at Toby and holding back the urge to cover myself. Victor patted the bed next to him and we both lurched forward.

"Redmond, stay."

I froze and my gut dropped to my feet. My heart skipped, rattled, flipped as Toby pranced over to the bed and hopped up beside him with all the vigor of a pampered lapdog. Victor gave him a rough scratch filled with affectionate words of encouragement, and Toby yipped in appreciation, landing belly-up across Victor's lap.

My throat tightened and stomach rolled as Victor's touches became more purposeful. Toby's head lolled back, and he went limp in his arms, surrendering to Victor's explorations and responding with little gasps. Victor dipped his head and Toby shivered as he brushed his lips down the line of his throat.

I released a low, plaintive whine.

"Shh." His eyes never lifted, the sound quick and sharp as a bullet. Sweat beaded at my temples and my cock throbbed as his hand drifted between Toby's legs. With slow, teasing strokes, he worked him up until he was gasping, hands balled in the bedding.

I couldn't take it. My body burned with the desire to have his hands on me, touching me, licking and biting and stroking me. Yet, every touch on Toby's skin stung me like fire ants and I had to bite the inside of my cheek to keep from screaming. I shouldn't have been jealous. It's not like I didn't know what they did together but making me watch was a new kind of torture, the collar around his neck an ever-present reminder of where I ranked.

Toby's eyes fluttered open and landed on me, pupils dilated and hazy. A lazy smile pulled across his face and he reached a hand toward me. "Can he play with us?"

"No."

"Why not?" he asked with a breathy whine.

"He's being punished."

"But I've been good," he said, rolling his body up into Victor with a lusty moan.

"Mmm."

"I want to play with him. Please?"

Victor paused his teasing, sucking in a deep breath. Toby peppered kisses along the line of his jaw, squeezing a *please* in between each one until he relented with a groan. Without looking up, he snapped his fingers in my direction and I jerked as if waking from a nightmare. Breathless, I went to drop to my knees.

"No. On your feet."

I blinked. Another denial. I wasn't even allowed to be his dog. Toby grinned and reached out to me as I walked upright to the side of the bed. He stroked my thigh and I swatted him away.

"Hands behind your back."

"But, sir—"

"Don't make me say it again."

Clutching my hands behind my back, I swallowed down bitter bile as Toby reached for me again. He dragged his fingers up my leg and over the curve of my ass. Head still hanging upside down, a lip tucked between his teeth, he traced my hip bone all the way to the base of my cock, eliciting an involuntary shudder.

Toby giggled and flipped himself over. "Ohhh, I want to taste him. Can I taste him?"

"Victor, please—"

"Fine," he answered as if I hadn't spoken at all. Toby wiggled with excitement, pulling himself onto all fours and crawling toward me.

"Please, Victor, I don't want—Ah, fuck." A white-hot spike shot through me as Toby ran his tongue across me from balls to head. This was bad. Real bad. Victor watched from behind Toby, his eyes firmly planted on his ass and palming himself through his pants. *God, fuck, just look at me.* Hands behind my back, at the whim of a man he didn't even like, I was lower than a dog. I was nothing. A piece of furniture unworthy of his attention.

Toby sucked me into his mouth and my knees nearly buckled. *Brakes, brakes, fucking brakes!* But I couldn't make myself say it. I deserved this. For the half-truths I'd told Katie. For the lies of omission to Sean. To be treated like I didn't exist.

Victor palmed himself harder, breath coming in little gasps. With a growl, he yanked open the drawer on the bedside table and extracted a condom and a bottle of lube. His hands shook as he shoved his pants off his hips and rolled on the condom. His hard shell cracked under the weight of his desire, but it wasn't for me.

He coated his cock and two fingers on his left hand with lube and then took a deep breath before coming up behind Toby on his knees. "You're a good boy, Toby," he said, running his right hand up the line of his spine. Toby arched up into his touch with a whine. His left hand went out of sight behind his ass. "Does he taste good?"

"Yes. *Yes!*" he said, pulling off me with a gasp and pushing back into Victor's hand. Tears pricked at the back of my eyes as his face contorted in pleasure, sweat making tracks down his forehead and dripping off his hair.

"Good. Make him come."

Toby wrapped his lips around me again as Victor squared himself up behind him. I felt more than saw what he did next. The hitch in Toby's breath, his moan vibrating through my cock.

My head spun, vision blurred. I wanted to obey Victor's order, I wanted to, but I couldn't. My hands came out from behind me, one clutching Toby's hair, the other on the edge of the bed to keep from falling. Every thrust from Victor sent my dick deeper down Toby's throat. He gagged, shuddered, clinging to my thighs with a bruising grip as Victor snapped his hips in an ever-quickening rhythm. I didn't want to come like this. Toby's eyes flicked up to mine and I saw the desperate need in his eyes. The need to please his Master.

"Tell me you're sorry, Redmond," Victor said, his breath ragged and voice hoarse.

"I'm sorry. Jesus, fuck, I'm sorry." I must have said it a hundred times as my orgasm threatened. The release I didn't earn or deserve. Victor's hand joined mine in Toby's hair as his hips stuttered and stilled.

Toby continued working over me, tired but determined. Victor leaned over his back and placed a kiss between his shoulder blades and whispering into his skin. *Come.* His cry muffled by my cock, his release splashed against my legs.

"Redmond...."

"No." I shook my head, sending beads of sweat flying. "Not like this. I want you."

Both of us bent over Toby's back; our heads were right next to each other. He took my chin in his hand, turned my face toward his, and kissed me, deep and possessive. His command written with teeth and tongue. My vision went white and with a cry, I unloaded into Toby's mouth.

"Fucking finally," Toby said, falling onto his side and flexing his jaw.

Tears streaming down my face, I fell to my knees. Muscles already tired from manual labor gave up entirely and only Victor's hands around my shoulders kept me from sliding to the floor.

"I'm sorry, I'm sorry, I'm so fucking sorry." I repeated the words like a mantra between heaving sobs.

"It's okay. Redmond, look at me," he said, sweeping a hand through my sweat-damp hair. I raised my eyes. I had no strength to lift my head. "I forgive you."

\* \* \*

"I didn't like that."

Victor and I sat facing each other in the bath, legs wrapped around each other's hips and my head resting on his shoulder. He ran warm water over my back with a natural sponge while I tangled my fingers in his long hair.

"Didn't like what?"

"You didn't touch me. You wouldn't look at me." Tears threatened again and I pushed my nose into the crook of his neck.

"I didn't like that either," he said with a deep sigh, "but I had to punish you."

"I know." I clung to him like a child, trembling and breathless. I didn't know when I'd become so dependent on him and it scared me.

"You going to tell me where you were?"

"It doesn't matter," I said. "It was stupid."

He kissed my shoulder. "Tell me anyway."

"I was...digging a hole." I laughed, face burning with embarrassment. "With my friend, Sean."

His back muscles tensed, and he pulled away. "Sean? Sean Delaney?"

"Yeah." Panic seized me as his face twisted into a sneer. *Idiot. You just told him you tried to blow him off for the only other gay guy in town.* "We're just friends. He doesn't even know—"

Victor stood up, making the water slosh out of the tub, and yanked a towel from the rack. He dried off with his back to me, his skin practically steaming.

"We're just friends, Victor, I swear."

He tied the towel around his waist, his shoulders rising and falling with a deep breath. He stomped out without a word, leaving me shivering and uncertain. Did I stay? Did I follow? Fucking hell, was he done with me entirely?

I leaped out of the tub and threw a towel over my shoulders before following as far as the doorway. We'd left Toby dozing in the bed tangled in a sheet, the bare expanse of his leg cutting a pale line down its center. His eyelids lifted only a little at Victor's entrance, pupils tracking his path while the rest of him remained melted to the mattress.

Victor dressed in silence and every passing second made my heart beat harder. I pulled the towel tight across my chest with one hand, the other curled around the door jamb. He didn't address me until after he'd snapped the clasp on his Rolex.

"How long have you been seeing him?" he asked. He faced me squarely, hands clasped loosely in front of him.

"I'm not seeing—" I cut myself off as his frown deepened. "We've only hung out a handful of times."

"And you didn't tell me."

"I didn't think—"

"You didn't think." His brow twitched, the rest of him hard as granite.

"I just watched you fuck another man and I'm not even allowed to have friends?" I asked, my frustration boiling over. "Two gay men can be in the same room without humping, you know."

His face jerked and I flinched. He took a step toward me and I took a step back, tripping over my own heels. Toby's eyes were fully open now and his lips curled in amusement.

"I'm sorry," I said quickly, my mouth dry.

Victor took a deep breath and his expression softened. "It's okay," he said. He traced his finger over the shell of my ear, leaving his hand resting on my cheek. "It's my fault. I haven't been honest with you. Or even myself. How could you have known?"

A tremble of apprehension went through me. "I don't understand..."

He brushed a kiss over my lips, featherlight and tremulous, before taking a step back toward Toby. He slipped his fingers into the boy's hair. Toby responded with a hum and a languid stretch that shifted his meager covering and left him bare. Victor urged him up onto his knees and he complied, all loose limbs and hooded eyes.

Adoration twisted into confusion as Victor slid his fingers over the buckle of Toby's collar. His breath caught as he pulled the leather free, that frantic energy coming alive again in his eyes.

"Victor—"

Victor shushed him and placed a gentle, chaste kiss on his forehead. He slipped the collar off his neck and Toby exploded into a fit of whines. He clutched at Victor's hands, pleading and begging, all of which Victor listened to with a cold patience.

"But I've been good," he insisted, his voice so broken and child-like it sent needles through my heart.

"Yes, you have." Victor kissed Toby's knuckles. He whimpered again as Victor let his hands drop and stepped back, the collar dangling from his fingers. He jerked his head toward the door. "Now, go on."

"Victor, please—"

Victor cut him off with a hard look. Toby crumpled, a hand going up to cover his eyes. A pained sound escaped him that made his whole body shake and when he looked up, the hurt in his eyes was so familiar my bones ached.

With a mumbled curse, Toby scrambled off the bed, snatched up his clothes, and stormed out without even bothering to put them on. Victor lifted his shoulders as if shrugging himself out of a heavy coat before turning back to me.

I stiffened, goose bumps rising on my damp skin. I couldn't take my eyes off the silver tag. The monogrammed *VI*.

"Are you ready for this, Redmond?" he asked, voice husky. He held the collar out between us just within reach. "You can tap the brakes if it's—"

"No." The word exploded from me before I could think and I grabbed his arm, tugging him a bit closer to me. Adrenaline zinged through me and I dropped my hand back to my side. "I mean, yes. I'm ready. I want it."

He smiled softly before lifting the collar up to my neck. It was soft and rough at the same time, just tight enough to make its presence known without being uncomfortable. The tag rested against my collarbone and I touched the cool metal with my fingertips.

"You're mine, now."

"Yessir." Everything felt light, dreamlike, and I swayed on my feet.

"And I'm yours." His voice hitched and it brought tears to my eyes. "Master and dog."

I fell headlong into that quiet space. I was his and he was mine. A commitment. A promise that I could lay my worries at his feet for him to carry. And in return, I would be loyal and true and shower him with the affection he so needed. I melted into his chest and he cradled me gently in his arms. His warmth seeped into my every cell, and I forgot we were two people until he took me by my shoulders and forced me back upright.

"From now on, you will check in with me," he said, his expression hard and commanding once again. "Anytime you leave the house. I don't care if it's to work, to the grocery store, or out with *Sean*." He sneered around Sean's name. "I want to know where you are and who you're with at all times. Got it?"

I nodded and my cock twitched. Unbelievable.

"Of course, you're allowed to have friends. You should have friends." He ran his thumb over my lower lip and then flicked the tag on my collar. "Just remember who you belong to."

He leaned in, lips stopping a hair's breadth from mine. I lifted my head, breath held and quivering in anticipation. He pulled back and I dropped dizzy back to earth.

"Yessir."

# Chapter 13

I was surprised by how easily I incorporated Victor's new rule into my life. I thought I'd be annoyed, but after the first day, I found his constant presence comforting, so much so I included him in even more of my decisions. What I wore, what I ate, what I watched on TV. He often responded with a simple thumbs-up or thumbs-down and I obeyed without question, confident in the knowledge he knew what was best for me.

And he rewarded me. God, did he reward me.

"So, when are you going to tell me who she is?" Sean asked.

"Hmm?" We were sitting on my tailgate watching the sun set over Sean's secret fishing hole, our bobbers dancing in the alternate patterns of light and shadow. I'd just texted Victor to ask how many beers I should have. His answer: three.

Sean gestured to my phone. "Your mystery lady."

"There's no lady." I dropped the phone next to my thigh. "It's nothing."

"Please. You don't shit without texting somebody. Whoever it is, it isn't nothing."

My cheeks heated and I took a small swig of my beer. I was already on number two.

"Fine," he said, rolling his eyes. "Keep your secrets. I won't tell you about the guy I've been seeing."

"Guy? What guy? When did this happen?"

"I'm. Not. Telling."

"Jesus, what are you, twelve?" I asked and he stuck out his tongue. "Look, it's not that I don't want to tell you..."

"Waiting for her to give you permission?"

"There are extenuating circumstances, okay."

Sean sighed and turned back to his fishing, giving the rod a little bounce. "Well, whoever she is, she's sure got you on a short leash."

*You have no idea.*

Sean gasped as my floater dipped below the waves and came back up half a second later. "Looks like you've got a hit."

I jumped up off the tailgate, both hands wrapped around my rod. "Shit. What do I do?"

"First off, calm down," he said with a laugh. He set his rod aside and stepped up behind me, resting his hands on my arms. "It was just a bump. You've gotta wait for it to take hold and—"

The floater went down again, and I yanked up on the rod, making Sean cry out and stumble backward. The catfish broke the surface with a great splash before bolting for deeper water. The line whirred, and I grasped at my spinning reel, the end of my rod bending dangerously toward the water.

"Whoa, you got it!" Sean appeared at my shoulder again, grinning like a schoolboy. "Now, just work it in. Easy, so you don't break the line."

I blew out a breath and pulled the rod up, forcing the fish closer to shore before reeling in the slack. "Fuck, it's strong," I said, biceps burning with the effort.

"You've almost got it. Keep going." Sean grabbed a net from the back of the truck and skipped toward the waterline, poised to snag the fish once it came closer to shore. Its big, brown back arched out of the water again and Sean whooped in excitement. Another pull and he got the net under it. "Got it!"

I dropped my rod, huffing and puffing. "How big is it?"

"Well, a leviathan it is not," Sean said, chuckling as he hooked his finger through the gills and lifted the fish from the net. "But you'll get a couple of good fillets out of it."

My heart sank at the sight of it. About eight inches long and as thick as Sean's wrist. He removed the hook and dropped the catfish, twitching and gasping, into a waiting bucket.

"You look disappointed," he said.

"I just expected more, I guess," I said. "It felt like pulling in a bulldozer."

Sean laughed. "Yeah, they always put up more fight than you'd expect. Fun though, right?"

I squatted down next to the bucket, filled with a strange sort of pride. The pride of a hunter. It may not have been a bear, but it proved I could provide for myself or my family if I needed to. My face tightened into a wide smile I couldn't stop.

When I looked up, Sean was watching me with a strange, wistful expression. "What?"

"Nothing," he said with a twitch as if I'd caught him with his hand in the cookie jar. He shuffled his feet, looked away, looked back. "Actually, would you go somewhere with me? Like, in public?"

I blinked and stood up. "Now?"

"No. Tomorrow. I have a...it's about my mother." His eyes pinched and he shoved his hands in his pockets. "I need to pick some things up from the executor of the estate. No big deal, it's just..."

His shoulders bowed inward and it squeezed my heart. An executor. Just one more reminder that his mother was gone. I wanted to be there for him. More than anything. But...

Frustration hardened his features as he followed my eyeline to my phone. "Are you fucking kidding me, Red? What, you have to ask for permission?"

"No, I—"

"You're my friend, probably my only friend, and I'm telling you I need you."

"Okay. I'm an asshole. I get it." I ran a hand over my face, releasing a long breath. "Fine. Yes. Of course, I'll go with you."

His posture relaxed a little, but the hurt lingered. The rear suspension creaked as he dropped back onto the tailgate and picked up his rod. I slid up next to him and picked at a spot of rust.

"I'm sorry."

"I know you are," he said with a sigh.

"You're not mad?"

"No." He laughed at my incredulous look. "What, you want me to be?"

"You probably should be."

"Yeah, probably." He pulled his lip between his teeth and kicked his feet. "There's no guy."

"What?"

"When I said I was seeing somebody, that was a lie. There's no guy."

"Oh."

"So, we're even."

"Because you lied?" I asked. "I don't think—"

"We're *even*," he said again, giving me a hard look.

I nodded, the corner of my mouth ticking up. "Okay. We're even."

\* \* \*

I was out in the garage when Victor called. I had the day off and decided to use the time to tinker around with my old Challenger, despite feeling more and more like it was a lost cause. The phone went off just as I'd busted my knuckles on yet another stripped bolt, unleashing a stream of curses that would make a sailor blush.

"Am I disturbing you?" Victor asked in response to my gruff answer.

"No. It's just this fucking car," I said, giving the tire a hard kick.

"It's not like you to call. Everything okay?"

"There's got to be something wrong for me to want to hear your voice?"

"No." I leaned back against the wall, my heart fluttering and a stupid grin pulling its way across my face. God, my tail was practically wagging.

"Can I give you a break? Take you to lunch?"

"Oh." My stomach sank. "Shit."

"Problem?"

"I know I should have asked you first..." Silence on the other end of the line as he waited me out. "I made plans. With Sean."

"Sean."

"Yeah. It's nothing, really. Some business with his mother's estate. He's been taking her passing pretty hard..."

"I see."

"I just wanted to be there for him, ya know."

"You're a good friend, Redmond."

For some reason, that didn't sound like praise.

"Okay," he said, and I disintegrated with relief.

"If you're looking for company," I started, digging my toe into the dirt, "maybe you should..."

"Should, what?" he asked, a tinge of irritation in his voice.

"Call Toby."

"Why would I do that?"

A little shock sizzled across my skin. "Because he needs it. He was pretty hurt by—"

"Relationships break up all the time, Redmond. It's not my job to take care of him anymore."

"Yeah, but—"

"What time are you meeting Sean?"

I sighed and massaged the space between my eyebrows. "Two o'clock."

"Good. I'm having something sent to you. Something for you to wear while you're out with Sean." He laughed darkly at my suspicious silence. "Don't worry. No one will know but you. I just want to be sure I am...on your mind."

"Y-yessir." I swiped at a line of sweat forming on my brow, my wagging tail now tucked firmly between my legs.

About an hour later, a courier pulled into my driveway bearing a package about the size of a shoebox. My pulse hammering a thunderous beat in my ears, I took it inside. I set the box down on the kitchen table and stared at it, mind reeling with a thousand horrific possibilities.

"Come on, Red. It's just another power play. It's probably nothing."

I grabbed a kitchen knife out of a drawer and returned to the box. I felt like Pandora preparing to unleash evils into the world. I flexed my fingers around the handle of the knife and took a deep breath before dragging it over the packing tape seal. The tape gave with a pop and the flaps sprang open.

I leaned over the open mouth of the box, muscles wound tight as if preparing to flee. Another small, slim box sat nestled inside. Black with a satin finish. The kind of thing you'd get in a high-end clothing store for your ties. I relaxed a little. Maybe that was it. Some innocuous piece of clothing designed to sit against my skin.

I lifted the black box out of its packaging. It was heavier, more solid than I expected. Definitely not a pair of socks. I gave it a shake. Nothing. I ran my fingers along the seam of the telescoping lid and the material squeaked as it rubbed against itself, releasing with a satisfying pop.

"You've got to be fucking kidding me."

A butt plug, cradled inside a nest of molded foam. My heart hammered against my ribs so hard, I had to sit down. *Something to wear...so he's on my mind.* I touched the elongated cone of smooth translucent silicone and pulled my hand back with a hiss as if it had stung me. Did he expect me to use this? To walk around with this thing inside me while I comforted my friend mourning the loss of his mother?

"Fuck that."

I pushed away from the table and turned my back on the evil thing. Too far. This was too far. It was one thing to torture me during our private sessions, but this was my life. By letting him govern over my choices, I'd already started wearing his collar in the real world. This was a line I wasn't sure I was ready to cross.

My body, however, was all in.

I pulled out my phone and opened my text messages, preparing to fire off a refusal, typed it out and everything, but froze with my thumb over the send button. My cock swelled and arousal hummed just beneath my skin. The thing tugged at me like a magnet. I imagined Victor's eyes darkening with pride and desire. How he would pet me and call me a good boy as he took everything that belonged to him.

I half-turned and glared sideways at the little box. I had an hour before I had to pick up Sean. Katie was out of the house, out with friends. I could...try.

"Jesus Christ, what am I thinking?" I muttered as I plucked the toy out of the box and rolled it around in my hands. Soft, flexible, just big enough to make a statement. I'd never used a butt plug before, and I had to admit a certain curiosity as the silicone flexed in my hand.

"Oh, what the hell."

Leaving my phone on the table, I took the toy and all its packaging with me into my bedroom. I closed my door and locked it behind me for good measure. I grabbed a bottle of lube from my bedside table. My heart raced and a hot flash of embarrassment coursed through me as I dropped my pants and positioned myself on the bed. Back against the headboard, knees pulled up to my chest and spread wide.

"Just relax." I took a deep breath and held it before releasing it slowly through my mouth. I coated the toy liberally with lube, dropping a little extra on the ends of my fingers. Holding my junk in one hand, I reached down with the other and prodded at my hole. It pinched around my finger and I took another deep breath, willing my muscles to relax.

I hissed through my teeth as one finger penetrated, then two, sending a tingling up through my balls. My body heated to my own touch as I worked my fingers inside me and prepared myself for that evil thing. I glared at the plug through hazy eyes, standing upright on my nightstand.

"All right, you sonofabitch," I growled, snatching it up. "Your turn."

I positioned the narrow tip against my hole and pushed. "Ah, God, Jesus, fuck!" My thigh muscles spasmed as the plug penetrated deeper, opening me up wider with every inch until it filled me. My insides burned and stretched and with one final push, it was fully sheathed inside me, the scalloped end the only thing keeping it from disappearing entirely.

It's not like I'd never been toyed before, I'd even bottomed before, but this was different. Instead of a rhythmic vibration or massage, the plug kept a constant and unrelenting pressure against my prostate. Heat unfurled inside me, making all my muscles quiver and my cock thicken. I eased my legs back down to the bed and my hips jerked as it rubbed, stretched, bent inside me.

"Ah, fuck, this is impossible," I said, panting and sweating as I gripped the bedding. I forced myself flat and tried to ignore the low hum building inside me. I thought about the weather, my car, my fucking taxes, anything but Victor and that goddamned plug inside me.

Little by little, my body cooled, and my cock deflated, still swollen but at a more tolerable level. I glanced at the clock at my bedside and cursed. Half an hour. Half an hour to get myself together and pick up Sean. With a groan, I eased myself upright. More stretching, more rubbing, more pressure. I hesitated at the edge of the bed and considered jerking off but decided against it.

Bending to retrieve my pants from the floor was a challenge and by the time I got them on, I was sweating. The head of my cock burned as it rubbed the inside of my jeans. I walked slowly, back hunched like an old man, every step making the silicone cone rub and push against my prostate.

"I can't do this. I can't. I should just cancel."

*But Sean.*

Warmth of a different kind flooded my chest as I thought of the not-quite-contained desperation in his eyes. He needed a friend, needed me, and God, I didn't want to let him down. Not this time. Not again.

With a growl of defiance, I peeled my pants back off and dropped onto my hands and knees. My muscles trembled and I took a series of long, deep breaths, my forehead lowered almost to the floor. A small bead of precome dropped from the head of my cock and I realized with a jolt I could come right here if I let myself.

I squeezed the base of my cock with a hiss. Was I really so far gone? Had I given him so much control I would fall apart at the mere idea of him standing over me while I shook and whimpered with want? My hole clamped down around the plug and my cock pulsed, the low hum of subspace filling my consciousness like water in a vase, and I bit the inside of my cheek to ground myself.

This was wrong. This day wasn't about what I needed. It was about what Sean needed. Victor had no place here.

A mournful sound slipped past my lips and I broke out in an all-over sweat as I reached behind me and pulled the thing free.

* * *

"Dude, are you okay?"

By the time I arrived at Sean's I was a mess. I hadn't let myself come, a small self-imposed punishment for my defiance, and the lack of release left me spiky and raw. Alternating hot and cold flashes made my teeth chatter and my head ache, and my semi-hard dick chafed against the inside of my jeans.

"I'm fine," I said, grip white-knuckle tight on the steering wheel. I'd spent the whole ride glaring at my phone in the seat next to me as if it were a loaded gun. Victor couldn't know I had gone against his order and yet I was sure the phone would ring at any second.

"You sure? You're all red and you look like you're gonna hurl." He raised the back of his hand to my forehead and I slapped it away.

"I said I'm fine. I'll be fine."

"If you're not feeling well—"

"I'm not blowing you off, okay. I'm not." The words came out barbed and he flinched. "Can we just go?"

"Yeah, okay."

We rode the whole way in silence, Sean staring at me like I had five heads as I bit into my cheek against wild spikes of arousal. Fucking Victor. He wasn't even here, and it was like he had a hand on my cock.

When we finally made it to the lawyer's office, I could hardly stay on my feet. I walked two steps behind Sean, knees wobbly and jerking like I had a palsy.

"Mister Delaney." Sean's lawyer greeted us enthusiastically as we entered. He took Sean's hand in a firm shake. Everything TV told you a lawyer should be. Pressed suit, slicked-back hair, shiny shoes. Even his smile didn't look real.

"Mister Dykowski." Sean returned the shake, tipped his head in my direction. "This is my friend, Red."

"Good to meet you, Red," he drawled, his accent the only thing betraying his small town origins. He extended his hand and I groaned as the force shook my whole body.

"He's not feeling well," Sean said in response to his concerned expression.

"I see." He wiped his hand on a handkerchief and gestured to a pair of chairs in front of a wide cherry desk. "Take a seat, gentlemen."

Sean sat, arching an eyebrow at me as I eased myself into the chair next to him, hunched and legs tightly crossed. The lawyer pulled out an accordion file full of documents and extracted a will along with a handful of other documents and a fat envelope marked with Sean's name in flowery penmanship. He gasped when he saw it.

"That's...my mother's..." His voice cracked and he swallowed hard.

The lawyer's eyes softened. "Yes. She left this for you with specific instructions that it is for your eyes alone."

He pushed the envelope across the desk toward Sean. Sean reached out for it, fingers trembling, but pulled back and pressed them against his lips. His shoulders heaved with ragged breaths and I leaned forward to touch them, stopping short as my cock pressed against my jeans. My stomach flipped and bile burned in the back of my throat.

*Don't forget who you belong to.*

"I'm sorry. I think I need a bathroom."

"Red—"

Sean's voice was strained and broken, and I cursed Victor again as I ducked out of the office and ran to the hallway bathroom. I burst into a stall just as my stomach upended and launched my lunch into the toilet. My whole world tipped on its axis. Sitting on the floor, head resting on the toilet, all I thought about was Sean. Sean sitting in that room alone suffering when I should have been next to him. Sean's shaking shoulders and tearful voice. *God, I'm an asshole.*

I'd let this thing with Victor get out of hand. I'd let a meaningless, sex-fueled relationship get between me and someone I actually cared about. And I did care about Sean, as much as I tried not to. Maybe more than I wanted to admit.

When I finally cleaned myself up and made it out of the bathroom, I found Sean sitting on a hard plastic chair in the hallway, expression rumpled, his mother's letter cradled in his hands like a delicate eggshell. He looked up as I approached, sniffing and running a quick hand over his face.

"You okay?" he asked in a rough voice.

"Yeah. Sorry. I think I just...ate something bad. You okay?"

He nodded and dropped his gaze back down to his hands, eyebrows pinched together.

I dropped down into the seat next to him. "Did you read it?"

"No. I don't think I'm quite ready for this, yet." He flipped the envelope over in his hand and sighed deeply. "Thank you for being here."

"For all the good I was. I spent most of the time in the bathroom."

"Well, it's the thought that counts," he said with a laugh. "Besides, you're here, now."

Warmth flowered in my chest and I stamped it down. "So, what now?"

"I have no idea."

"Wanna get drunk?"

"God, yes."

# Chapter 14

Wе stopped off at a liquor store for a liter of cheap tequila and a fifth of good whiskey. Sean had arranged some lawn furniture around our little fire pit and half an hour later, we were sweating beside a roaring flame. The tequila chilled in a bucket of ice at our feet as we sipped on whiskey, the only sounds the clink of ice in our glass and the shift and crack of burning brush.

Sean didn't speak of his mother, didn't speak of anything really, though I could tell by the lines around his mouth she was on his mind. Every third or fourth sip, his glass would get caught halfway to his lips as if he'd forgotten for a moment where he was and what he was doing, sometimes for so long I almost reached out and touched him to get him started back up again.

"I have an idea. Let's play a game," he said. We'd made it about halfway down the bottle of whiskey and that combined with the heat gave his face a rosy glow.

"What sort of game?"

He reached down for the tequila bottle at our feet and dropped it heavily on the table between us. "Twenty questions."

"And what's that for?" I asked, gesturing with my glass toward the bottle.

"Lubricant," he answered with a wink. He grabbed my glass and tossed the dregs of both our drinks in the fire, making the flames jump and sputter, before pouring a heavy measure of tequila into each one. "We'll take turns asking each other questions. If one of us asks a question and the other answers, they drink."

"And if you ask something I don't want to answer?"

"You drink."

"Sounds like an awful lot of drinking."

"That's the idea," he said with a devilish grin. I scowled at the yellowish liquid sliding around my glass, cringing as the sharp smell burned my nose. "I'll start easy. How old were you when you lost your virginity?"

The question caught me by surprise, triggering a laugh that nearly knocked my chair over. "That's easy?"

He shrugged. "It's not fun if it's not a little scandalous." He leaned toward me, eyebrows bouncing. "So?"

"Sixteen."

He pursed his lips into a little *oh* and dropped his chin in his hand as if waiting for more.

"I answered your question. Now, drink."

He clicked his tongue. "Fine." He threw his drink back in one go, coughing and groaning as it went down. "Jesus Christ, that's awful."

"My turn," I said, another laugh bubbling up from my toes. I squinted at him as I refilled his glass. "When did you know you were gay?"

"Let's see." He sat back in his chair, eyes pointed at the sky and ankles crossed. "The cliché is to say I always knew, but that's not really true. I mean, I noticed other boys, but never really equated it to anything sexual. It just wasn't an option. Until..."

"Until?"

"Do you really wanna hear this?" he asked, giving me a sideways look.

"I asked, didn't I?"

"There was this guy," he said with a sigh. "An old family friend. We practically grew up together. He spent a semester abroad in high school. I didn't see him for three whole months and when he came back it was like a switch flipped inside me. He seemed so... different. Grown up. And fucking *hot*."

We both laughed. "So, did you—"

"Ah—" Sean waved a finger at me and tapped the rim of my glass. I rolled my eyes and tossed the liquor back, unloading a string of curses as it burned its way past my sternum. "And yes. We did."

"Was he your first?"

"That's another question."

I snatched up the bottle, refilled my glass, and waited.

"Yes, he was my first."

I lifted my glass in a salute. The second shot tasted marginally better than the first.

"My first time was awful," I said, coughing around the shitty booze. My body turned heavy and liquid, like I was melting into the chair. "My entire sex education came from an old *Playboy* I found in the back of my dad's closet. I barely knew what went where."

"Were you in love with her?"

"God, no."

We both laughed before dropping into a companionable silence. The sun sank low, painting the sky red, and I imagined we were on Mars. Lost and building our own civilization in an alien desert. In that world, I could tell him the truth. I'd only slept with a girl in a desperate attempt to be something I wasn't. And I wanted him to know. I wanted him to know so bad my bones ached, but even though I knew he was the one person in the world who wouldn't judge me, I couldn't make myself say the words.

"Are you lonely?"

The question fell from my lips like lead and sat heavy between us. Our game had lost all form and, even though it wasn't his turn,

Sean tipped his drink back before pressing the empty glass to his forehead. He didn't have to answer. It rolled off him in waves.

"Shit, I'm sorry," I said.

"It's okay—"

"No, this is supposed to be fun and I fucked it up, I think."

He laid his hand on my forearm, sending a rush of heat through my chest not unlike when he'd touched my leg on that first night on the river. Only this time I didn't pull away. My own loneliness opened up like a great black pit inside me. *Tell him. Just tell him.* He leaned toward me and I leaned toward him until we were dangerously close.

"I just can't seem to do anything right around you," I said.

"You do more right than you think."

He smiled and it sent every drop of tequila straight to my head. I couldn't stop gazing at the curve of his lips, the little crease that formed in the corner of his mouth. I laid my hand over his, soft and smooth and so completely opposite from mine.

We both jumped and I cursed loudly as my phone went off in my pocket. Barking dogs. Great.

"You need to go?" Sean asked, a touch of disappointment in his voice.

"No." I silenced the ringtone and tossed my phone on the table without looking at it. I fell back into my chair, arms crossed tight over my chest and a scowl pulling at my features.

"Everything okay?"

"Yes. No. I don't know." I ran a hand over my face with a tired sigh. "I got into this thing because I thought it would be simple, ya know? Casual. More of an arrangement than a relationship."

"And now?"

"It is so fucking far from simple."

"So, what? She wants more?" His eyes narrowed and my expression twitched. "*You* want more?"

"No," I said quickly. My shoulders dropped and I shook my

head, the tequila making my brain slosh around in my skull. "I don't know. Sometimes, I think maybe I do, but then there are times when I think the whole thing was a mistake to begin with."

"It's because you're lonely," he declared with a triumphant grin, pointing at me with his glass and making the contents splash over his hand.

I laughed. "You're drunk."

"Yes, but that doesn't mean I'm wrong." He relaxed back into his chair, head lolling back and face to the sky. "Lucky for you, I'm here. We can be lonely together."

"Yeah," I said. "Lucky me."

# Chapter 15

"What trouble are you into now, Red?"

Bo slapped his big hands against the fender of the Toyota Camry I was working on, making the whole cab shake and sending the tools I had perched on the engine careening into the compartment.

"What are you talking about?"

"First, you bring that pervert's car in here—"

"Hey—"

"Now, I've got a police officer in the front office making everyone nervous."

I blinked. "Police?"

He leaned his bulk toward me, bringing us nose to nose. "Are we going to have a problem, Red?"

I cocked my head to peer over his shoulder at the bank of windows leading into the front office. Sure enough, a dark-blue back stood framed in it, surrounded by the unmistakable air of authority. My heart dropped.

*Katie.*

"I'll take care of it." I wiped my hands on a shop rag and headed toward the office at a trot. The officer turned as I burst through the door, thumbs hooked in his utility belt and eyes hidden behind mirrored aviators.

"Whatever she did, I'm sure we can work it out," I panted. "If she broke something, or stole something..."

The officer didn't reply, a smug smile creeping across his face. Something familiar in his expression made me pause. My eyes skimmed over his uniform. Not Black Creek police. City of Kilgore. He slid his aviators down his nose, revealing hazel eyes rimmed in long, dark lashes. The tag on his chest just above his badge read *R. Tobias.*

I choked. "Toby."

His grin lengthened and I had to steady myself against the wall to keep from falling. He was barely recognizable in his police blues, his mannerisms tightly controlled and face devoid of makeup.

"W-what are you...what are you doing here?"

His smile faltered. "I'm here for what you stole from me."

"What I stole?" I ground out the words through gritted teeth. "I didn't steal—"

"You took him from me." He took a step toward me, his voice tight and barely controlled. My eyes swung around the empty office, the closed door. Fuck, this was bad.

"We should take this outside."

"It took me a year to earn his trust." His eyes welled and his voice shook. "Then you waltz in with your chiseled jaw and broken eyes—"

"What are you gonna do? Arrest me?" My temper flared, sending fire through my veins. "You're a little out of your jurisdiction, Officer Tobias."

"He won't talk to me. Won't look at me."

"And what do you think he'll do if he finds out you turned up here? Or anyone else, for that matter. You'd never be allowed in that house again."

He rocked back on his heels as if I'd struck him. His composure shattered. His hands shook and shoulders heaved with deep, ragged breaths. Dark circles were painted under his eyes and I wondered if they'd always existed, hidden under his makeup, or if recent events had put them there.

Hyperaware of the window at my back, I took him by the arm and tugged him outside. He'd parked his cruiser right in front and I leaned him back against it. He seemed so fragile, as if he might crumble in my hand like he was made of sugar. The sassy, confident boy had been replaced by a man on the edge. Tired. Desperate. Scared. Like me, he lived his life playing a role and I'd taken the one thing from him that was real.

"I need him," he whimpered.

"I know."

"I can't take care of myself. I can't."

"Yes, you can." I took him by the shoulders and forced him up straight. "He wouldn't have let you go if you weren't ready."

He closed his eyes a moment and took a deep, shuddering breath. When they opened again, they were eerily calm. He pulled himself up, shrugged me off, and slipped his aviators back over his eyes.

"I see why he likes you," he said in a flat voice.

"Why's that?"

The corner of his mouth quirked, but he didn't answer. He turned his back to me, opened the door of his cruiser, and slipped inside. I stepped back, expecting him to pull away, but he just sat there, hands draped loosely on the steering wheel.

"Red!"

I jumped as Bo shouted my name from the garage. He stood in the bay door, arms crossed over his barrel chest and glaring a hole into my forehead. With a final glance back at Toby, I crossed the parking area toward him.

"We gonna have a problem?" he asked.

"No, sir. It was just a misunder—"

*Bang!*

My blood went cold as a gunshot rang through the parking lot. I spun around back toward Toby's cruiser. The inside was still, the view through the windshield marred by a splash of red.

"Fuck."

Before I was even aware of my actions, I was standing next to the driver's side window. The entire window was painted a sickening crimson. A hole the size of a golf ball punctured the upper corner, the laminated glass shattered in a spiderweb pattern and barely held together. I jerked at the door, but it was locked, so instead I thrust my fingers through the hole and yanked until the whole window pulled out in a crumpled sheet.

"Jesus Christ, Toby, what did you do?"

Toby lay back in his seat, clutching a hole in his cheek. His gun lay between his feet, the barrel wet and glistening with gore. I wadded up my shop rag and pressed it to his face in an effort to stop the blood flowing down his neck and chest. He pushed me away weakly, spraying me with a wet, choking cough.

"Jesus, fuck." Lawrence appeared behind me, his hands in his hair.

"Call an ambulance," I barked. Lawrence fumbled for his phone and spewed information to the operator in a panic-stricken voice. I cradled Toby's head against my chest as his body shuddered and went limp. "Come on, stay with me. I know it hurts. I know it does." I stuttered as a sob forced its way up my throat. "Just don't give up, okay? Please don't give up."

\* \* \*

I sat on a gurney in the emergency room, my shirt sticking to me, staring at my own bandaged hands. I hadn't even noticed the deep gashes in my palms until the paramedic pulled me aside. They'd already whisked Toby away in an ambulance and left me standing numb next to his blood-spattered cruiser.

"How are you doing, Mister Cole?" A nurse appeared at my side, getting my attention with a gentle touch on my arm.

"My hands won't stop shaking." My voice sounded hoarse and I swallowed thickly.

"It's the adrenaline," she said. "It'll pass in a few minutes. I can give you something to help calm you down if you like."

I shook my head. "Is he..."

"He's alive. The bullet exited through his cheek. Shattered his jaw, lost a lot of blood, but he should pull through. He's lucky."

"Yeah. Lucky."

"Does he have any family nearby? Someone we can call?"

I blinked and let my hands drop to my thighs. "I...I don't..."

"What about Victor Itachi?" My heart jerked. "He's listed as his emergency contact, but we can't seem to reach him."

"Son of a bitch," I said under my breath.

Her expression softened and questions flickered behind her eyes, but she didn't press. "There's an officer here from Kilgore who wants to ask you some questions if you're up for it."

"Sure. Fine." I ran a hand over my eyes. "Can I make a phone call, first?"

"Of course. They're in the waiting room when you're ready."

She gave me a pat on the knee before scooting away to help other patients. I grabbed my phone and pulled up Katie's cell phone number. The last thing I wanted was for her to hear about this on the news.

"Hey, it's me," I said when the voicemail picked up. "Something pretty major went down at the shop. I'm fine, but I'll probably be tied up for a while. So, don't freak out, okay? I'll call you when I can. Love you, kiddo."

I clicked off and started shaking all over again. *I know it hurts.* It wasn't hard to imagine the place Toby was in when he pulled that trigger. The fear and desperation he must have felt. We weren't so different after all. How far would I have gotten without Victor? How far would I get after he was gone? Would it even matter to him?

My phone lit up with a text notification from Sean.

*I SWEAR TO GOD, IF YOU'RE DEAD, I'M NEVER SPEAKING TO YOU AGAIN!*

I laughed and plucked out a reply.

*News travels fast. I'm not dead. I'll call you later.*

I dropped my phone onto the gurney and released a long breath, some of my melancholy leaving with it.

# Chapter 16

After talking with the police, I went straight to the plantation. I brought the collar with me, but left it tucked in the glovebox of my truck. I sat in the driveway, stomach writhing like an angry snake, and stared up at the glowing windows. What would I do? Katie's face as she raved about her new school flashed in my mind, making my eyes burn. I knew what I *should* do, but my life had become so entangled in my relationship with Victor, there would be no separating it without consequences.

One thing was for certain. I needed to be a man today. I needed to be strong, to not bend or fall on my knees. My refusal to wear Victor's collar was a statement in itself and the thought made my skin cold and my palms clammy. I fought the urge to go back for it with every step. I felt naked in a very true sense, my hand fluttering up to my neck as if to hide my bareness.

I paced at the base of the stairs. The doorman's beady eyes tracked me back and forth, back and forth, but he remained silent. I'd thrown a jacket on over my soiled shirt and held it closed over my chest, my knuckles white where they clenched in the fabric.

He squinted through the peephole at the light, metallic tap of

129

the knocker. "He's here," he grumbled over his shoulder at me. I halted my pacing as the door swung open.

I imagined this is what Lucifer must look like. The light bearer, fallen angel, both beautiful and dangerous. My heart jerked so violently at the sight of him, I thought it might pull loose from its moorings and fly from my mouth.

"Redmond." His voice was hard but held a note of surprise. His eyes jerked down to my bare neck, then to my bloodied shirt. An expression of genuine sadness and regret flashed across his face. Quick as a blink and then gone.

"You should have called him," I said, fighting past the tightness in my throat.

The corners of his mouth pulled downward. "Is he okay?"

"He's alive," I said. "He is not okay."

His eyes lowered and his shoulders drooped. "He's always been a troubled boy. Even before—"

"Don't."

He blinked. "Don't what?"

"Make excuses like you didn't play some part in this."

His eyes hardened and he took a step toward me. I sucked in a breath, back rod straight and head high. The silence between us pricked like needles as he glared at me, still as a statue. Sweat ran down the back of my neck, but I would not break.

He gestured to the stairs behind me. "Let's talk in private, shall we?"

I released my held breath and headed up the stairs. My back tingled with his presence behind me. Since that first time, I had only ever climbed these stairs on the end of a leash and the reversal was dizzying.

He slipped past me once we reached the door to our room to let us in and I waited in the entryway as he lowered himself primly into a chair. Just an ordinary armchair, but it looked like a throne with him in it. He rested his elbows on the armrests, fingers steepled under his nose and eyebrows raised.

"I can't do this anymore." The words were brittle on my tongue and broke as they left my lips. "Not like this."

He took in a deep breath and released it slowly before dropping his hands to his lap. "This is about Toby."

"It's about me. You crossed a line. With that...package." My voice gained solidity as I clung to the discomfort, the inappropriateness.

"How's that?"

"With *jealousy*." I took a step toward him, fists clenched, teeth bared.

His eyebrow arched and lips curled. "You think I'm jealous of Sean Delaney?"

"Why else would you do something like that? Intrude on our time together?"

"I had to push you. It's what you needed."

"That was a hard day for him. He needed me to be present and I wasn't because of you."

"You could have just said no," he said with a small laugh that sent shots of adrenaline through my brain. "You always have a choice, Redmond."

"Do I?" Angry tears pricked at the back of my eyes. "Because you seem to be making a lot of my choices for me, lately."

His mirthful expression sagged. He stood up out of his throne and I took a step back. I had to maintain distance, or I would crumble.

"It's my own fault," I said. "I've given too much of myself to this...whatever it is. I need something real."

"This isn't real?" He stepped toward me again, advancing until my back pressed against the wall and I could no longer retreat. He lifted his hand to my cheek, and I shrank away. He was so close. My eyes were drawn to his lips, those pretty lips that inspired such fantasies.

"I want to tell him," I said, spewing the words before I could back out. "About everything. About...me."

He pulled back. "Why?"

"Because he's my friend and I'm lying to him." The tears that threatened earlier sprang forth again, this time unstoppable. "Because I'm tired of living in half measures. Of holding myself back because I'm afraid of what people will see. Because I don't want to end up like Toby when you're done with me."

He sucked in a sharp breath. His hand rose to my cheek again and this time I leaned into it, sagged into it, gripping his forearm in case he saw fit to snatch it away again. That dreadful black hole of loneliness opened in me again. In moments like this, I could love him, wanted to love him, anything to fill that awful blank space.

"I need more," I said hoarsely. "More than games and power play. More than this place."

"And you think you can get it from Sean Delaney?"

"I think I want it from you."

There it was. An admission I wasn't prepared for and it disarmed us both. Victor's face hardened and he took a step back. You could fit infinity in that small distance. I clung to his shirt as he extracted himself from my grip and fell into his armchair. No longer a throne. The man in it just a man filled with the same loneliness and regrets.

"I can't, Redmond." His shoulders drooped and his hands fell limply on the armrests.

"Why not?"

"You know why."

"But you said it yourself," I said, taking a step toward him. "We don't have to be afraid."

He sat up straighter, his brows pulled low over his eyes. "Do you know anything of my life outside this place?"

"Only because you've never told me."

"Right." He stood so fast, it made me flinch. Fists clenched but still shaking. The skin around his collar darkening with an angry flush. My strong Master was starting to crack and my nerves jangled with alarm.

"I know you pretend to be strong," I said, voice shaking, "but you've given all of them control over you."

His eyes shot open wide and the air went sharp as a whip crack. I trembled under the heat of his glare.

"You ungrateful cur." He spat the words from between clenched teeth. "After everything I've done for you."

"I'm sorry. I'm sorry." I dropped to my knees in front of him, head bowed. My heart pounded in my ears and my hand lifted to my bare neck again. This was wrong. Collar or no, I was still his dog, whining and begging for forgiveness. Wanting only affection. Cowering under his wrath. I reached out to touch him, he grabbed me by the wrists and—

*Smack!*

A spray of needles across my right cheekbone followed by a wash of heat from my ear to my collar. My right eye watered, blurring his image as he stood over me, shoulders rising and falling with heavy breaths. His shadow leaned toward me and just like that, I was fifteen again. My muscles froze, my chest collapsed in on itself, my vision blurred.

"B-brakes!"

As if I were a sorcerer and I'd uttered some magic word, he froze. Slightly bent, arm outstretched and hand open as if about to snatch me up. He blinked once and then rocked back on his heels, his face going slack.

One hand pressed against the hot skin of my cheek, I scrambled upright. Something shattered inside me with the force of his blow, some fragile hope, and it lay in pieces at our feet. Eyes lowered, I dragged my heavy limbs toward the door. He called my name once, softly, and broken in the middle.

* * *

Sean's door flew open the instant I knocked, despite the late hour. I'd used the privacy of the drive between the plantation and Sean's house to have a proper emotional breakdown and now I stood on his doorstep, eyes raw and rumpled. He answered in his boxers, a robe hastily thrown over his shoulders and hair sticking out. His eyes bounced from my blood-spattered shirt to the welt on my cheek.

"I'm sorry," I said, voice gravelly with emotion. "I just...I didn't want Katie to see me like this. I didn't know where else to go."

"Jesus, Red." He threw his arms around my neck, pulled me into a tight hug, and I melted into it. He released me and pulled me inside by my shoulders, ushering me into the kitchen. He shoved me into a stool at a high-top table before rushing to the freezer for a bag of peas. My head ached from crying and I propped it up on my knuckles. Sean dragged another stool closer to me and pulled himself into it before pressing the peas against my bruised cheek. With his free hand, he rubbed slow circles on my back.

I leaned into his touch, laying my hand over his. Despite the makeshift ice pack, it felt warm. He didn't ask what happened. He didn't say anything, he was just there, and that great yawning pit inside me didn't seem quite so scary or so cold.

"I'm so fucking stupid," I said after a long silence.

"What are you talking about?"

Tears pressed against the back of my eyes again and I squeezed them shut. "You were right."

"About what?"

"About everything. I wanted more. I *want* more. I want all

those things you see in Lifetime movies. Walks on the beach, picnics in the park, fucking white picket fences. All of it."

"That doesn't make you stupid," he said. "Everyone wants that. Hell, I want that."

"But we can't have that."

"Is this your near-death experience talking?"

"I'm serious, Sean."

"Yes, *you* can," he said firmly. "You think you're this miserable wretch, but you're a good person, Red. You deserve—"

"I can't." I slapped my hands on the table, making him jump, the bag of peas dropping with a wet slap on the table.

"Why not?"

I took a deep breath, eyes on my clenched fists. "For the same reason as you."

He stiffened, the only sound a sharp intake of breath. My heart seized and part of me wanted to snatch the words out of the air, to reel them back in and pretend I'd never said them. He stood stiffly and turned his back to me.

"Shit, Red," he said on an exhale.

"I'm sorry," I said, shoulders dropping nearly to the table.

"For what, exactly?"

"For not telling you. For not trusting you."

"So, this whole time—the blowing me off, being afraid to be seen with me—that was all what? Fear of being outed?"

"Told you I'm fucking stupid," I said with a dry laugh. Tears threatened again and I picked up the bag of peas and pressed it against my eyes. A chair scraped across the hardwood and he wrapped his hands around mine. He tried to tug them away, but I held fast.

"Come on, Red, look at me."

I shook my head, clutching the bag even tighter.

"Why not?"

"I'm afraid," I said, voice ragged. "You're my friend and I've been hiding this from you."

"I'm not angry, Red," he said. He wrapped his arms around my shoulders and pulled me into him. "I'm just sad you had to go through this alone."

"I do trust you," I said. I wilted into his arms, his strong, steady heartbeat thumping in my ear. "I'm just a coward. God, I'm so fucking tired of being scared all the time."

"I know," he said, the same weariness leaking into his voice. "I told you that chicken suit is the worst."

We both laughed and I burrowed deeper into his chest. He rocked me gently and the tension I'd been carrying since the day we met leaked away. It felt good to let it go, to trust him. For the life of me, I couldn't figure out why I hadn't told him sooner. Of course, he understood. He'd been here before.

"He was like me, ya know. Scared and alone."

"You're not alone."

I smiled against his chest. "Yeah, I know."

"So, I have to ask," he said. "The barking dogs..."

I tensed and pulled myself upright. "Victor," I answered around the rock in my throat.

"Are you in love with him?"

"No. Maybe. I don't know," I said, scrubbing a hand across my face and hesitating over the mark on my cheek. "I think I wanted to be in love with him."

"Wait. He did this to you?" Sean asked. I nodded and his expression hardened. "Son of a bitch."

"It's not as bad as it seems," I said, but even to me, the words sounded wrong. "Our relationship isn't exactly...conventional."

"It doesn't matter."

"I broke the rules and he punished me. He went too far, sure, but when I said the word, he stopped."

"What, like a safe word?"

I nodded, a spike of embarrassment coloring my cheeks. I turned my face away and he grabbed me by my shirt, forcing me to look him in the eye.

"He shouldn't have hit you," he said. "Not if it makes you feel like this. He should make you feel safe. Cared for."

"I do feel safe," I insisted, but my voice tremored around the words. I did feel safe. Safer than I had in a long time. But the protective walls he'd built around me were made of glass and they shattered the moment he struck me, leaving me raw and exposed.

Sean sighed deeply and stood up again. He returned moments later, dropping our half-empty bottle of tequila in the center of the table with a loud *thonk*.

"It's a little late for twenty questions," I said.

"You planning on sleeping?" he asked, pouring two glasses of the foul stuff and pushing one toward me. I shook my head. "Okay then. I'll go first." He lifted his glass, a sly grin spreading across his face. "So, Red. When did you know you were gay?"

\* \* \*

I woke up with the distinct impression I wasn't where I should be. My head ached and my eyelids stuck together. Something soft and warm vibrated at a low frequency beneath me. A rhythmic swell like being at sea. I pushed my nose into it, filling my lungs with a light, comforting smell. It shifted beneath me, making a small sound of contentment. Only then did I realize it was a person.

I shot upright, making my hungover brain slosh around in my skull and nearly falling backward out of the couch. Sean lay stretched out beneath me, hair mussed and cheeks pink, his even breathing undisturbed by my sudden motion. He was shirtless and in his boxers, prompting me to do a quick mental tally of my clothes.

Shirt. Check.

Pants. Check.

Socks. Check, check.

After a small sigh of relief, I carefully peeled myself away while searching my memory of the night before. My face heated as I remembered my sloppy confession. Everything got fuzzy once the drinks started flowing, blacking out completely after a drunken stumble to the couch. The empty bottle and both glasses lay on the floor beside it like evidence in a crime scene photo.

I glanced at my watch. Fuck, 7:00 a.m. I got up from the couch, wobbling with the last dregs of drunkenness, and felt my way through the low light to the bathroom. Closing the door first so as not to wake Sean, I clicked on the light. I froze at the sight of my own haggard reflection. Eyes red-rimmed and puffy. A dark-red bruise coloring my cheekbone. I poked at its edge and a tingling ache spread through the side of my face.

My stomach flipped and I had to grip the sink to keep from falling. What had I done? I'd stepped out of line and I'd been punished. Given the nature of our relationship, his reaction should have been expected, but it caught me off balance. As my vision blurred, I had seen the Colonel standing over me. When his hand rose, my trust in him had turned to fear, deep and primal.

I splashed cold water on my face and once my stomach had settled back into its proper position, I clicked off the light and slipped back out to the living room. With my boots hooked in my fingers, I tiptoed past the couch to the front door.

"Red?"

I stopped, hand on the knob, at the sound of Sean's voice, slurred and gravelly with sleep. I turned to find him squinting at me, face scrunched up.

"You leaving?" he asked.

"Yeah," I answered. "Katie's probably looking for me. You okay?"

He groaned in response, rolling onto his side and curling into a tight ball. He looked so vulnerable in that big sofa all alone, skinny legs pulled all the way up to his chest. I dropped my shoes in the entryway and grabbed a throw blanket off the back of a chair as I made my way back toward him. He hummed in gratitude when I draped it over him, curling his fingers around the edge and pulling it up to his nose.

"I'm sorry," I said, throat tight, "for barging in on you last night and dumping all that shit on you."

"Don't be sorry," he said without opening his eyes. "I'm relieved, actually."

I laughed. "Relieved? Why?"

"'Cause at least I don't have a crush on a straight guy."

My heart rate jumped a tick, sending a warm rush of blood to my face. "You have a crush on me?"

"Don't get a big head about it. I haven't been laid in a long time." He laughed, followed by another groan, and pushed his nose deeper into the cushions. "Shit, I think I'm still drunk."

"It's okay. Go back to sleep." I tucked the blanket tighter around him and he burrowed into it. His breathing turned into light snores within seconds. A piece of hair stuck out from the top of his head and I brushed my fingers through it. Soft and just long enough it wanted to curl.

It was weird. For all my rush to leave, I found it hard to pull myself away.

\* \* \*

"Where the fuck have you been?"

I hadn't even made it fully through the door before Katie's voice slammed into me, making my soggy brain spasm. "Language," I groaned. "And volume. I've had a long night."

"You've had a long night?" she asked, advancing on me with fire in her eyes. "What about my long night worrying if my brother was ever coming home? I called you like a million times."

I'd turned off my phone in case Victor tried to call.

"Sorry," I said. "Phone died."

Katie eyed me with that look that reminded me so much of the Colonel. I ducked my head and made for the fridge and a bottle of water. Maybe if I didn't look at her, she'd go away.

"What happened?"

Nope.

"Can we talk about this later?"

"No." She slapped the refrigerator door closed, making me stumble backward.

"Just give me a break, Kaitlyn," I snapped, making her pull back. "I'm tired, I'm hungover, and I don't want to talk about it, okay?"

She blinked, eyes welling, features pulled into a tight knot. The last of my drunkenness burned away, leaving me with a three-alarm headache that made my vision blur, and I leaned over the sink to regain my balance.

"What's going on with you, Red?" she asked. No longer the strong voice of a woman, but the quivering uncertainty of a girl and it burrowed into the cracks in my heart. "I get this weird voicemail from you and you sounded so..." Her chin wobbled and her eyes pinched. "And then, I hear about a shooting at your garage and you don't come home..."

She trailed off into a stream of sniffles. I wrapped my arms around her and she buried her face into my chest, her hands clutching the back of my shirt. Tears pricked at the back of my eyes as I peppered the top of her head with kisses.

"It's okay. I'm okay."

"Where were you?"

"Nowhere. Fuck, I'm an asshole."

"Worst big brother ever." She pulled back a step, wiping her nose with the back of her hand. "But I'm glad you're not dead."

"Me too," I said with a dry laugh, brushing the tears from her cheeks. A horn sounded from outside. "Your ride is here. You should get going or you'll be late for school."

She sniffed and I didn't look up until her scraping footsteps reached the door. She paused there a moment, head down, face mostly hidden behind her auburn hair.

"You're all I have, you know," she said and out of the door she went.

# Chapter 17

A knock at the door startled me awake. For a disoriented moment, I thought I was still on Sean's plush leather sofa but the spring poking into my ribs brought me back to reality. Each rap sent a needle through my temple. Had Bo sent someone over to drag me to work? I vaguely remembered calling in sick before crashing on the couch, but it still wouldn't surprise me.

Another barrage of knocks, this time coupled with a voice. "Delivery!"

"Whatever it is, I don't want it," I barked before shoving my head beneath a scratchy throw pillow. More knocking. "Fuck off!"

"Come on, man, don't bust my balls," came the plaintive voice again. "I just need a signature."

I growled and forced myself to my feet. I yanked the door open, wincing in the glare of the afternoon sun. A kid in an oil-stained shirt and a baseball cap shoved a clipboard into my hand. A patch on his hat read "East Texas Automotive Supply."

"You sure you're in the right place?" I asked, squinting over his shoulder at a wooden crate being offloaded into my driveway.

"That you?" he asked, gesturing to my name and address on the waybill.

"Yeah."

"Then, I'm in the right place."

"But I didn't order—"

"Look, I just drive the truck," he said, "and I'm running behind. Just sign the form, will ya?"

I scowled and scratched my name on the bottom of the form. With a sarcastic thank-you, the kid tore off the carbon copy, handed it to me, and jogged back to his truck, leaving me standing befuddled in my driveway. I scrubbed at my eyes, sure I must be in some kind of hangover nightmare, but the crate was still there.

"What fresh hell is this?"

I walked a wide circle around the box as if something might pop out and attack me. Just a normal wooden shipping crate about the size of a freezer and stamped all over with Fragile, This Side Up. A little pouch containing a packing list was stuck to the top. I peeled it off and retrieved the slip of paper inside it.

*Contents: Qty 1 Engine for 1970 Dodge Challenger*
*Ship to: Redmond Cole*
*Bill to: Victor Itachi*

"Son of a bitch."

I wadded up the papers in my hands and threw them at the half-open door of the garage. They bounced off the dilapidated Challenger's nose. In one of my weaker moments, which were many around him, I'd told Victor all about the car and what it meant to me. Now, he was using it. Turning my dream into just another power play.

Heart thundering in my ears, I whipped out my phone and scrolled down to his number. He answered on the second ring. "What the hell is this?" I growled into the receiver before he could even get out a greeting.

"Oh, good. You got my gift," he answered coolly.

"Cut the shit. What are you up to?"

"I'm not up to anything, Redmond," he said, voice smooth as

ever, and the loyal dog inside me shivered. "I just wanted to make amends for my behavior last night."

"It'll take more than a car engine."

"It's what you need, isn't it?" he asked.

"I told you what I needed," I said through gritted teeth, "and you hit me."

Silence stretched between us, long and heavy, twisting my insides into knots. "Do you want this to be over, Redmond?" he asked gently. "To put the brakes on for good?"

The thought made my knees weak and I sank to the ground right there in the driveway, my back against that evil crate.

"Go to dinner with me," he said.

"Is that a command?"

"No. A request. No expectations. Just food and...conversation."

"Sounds like a date."

"Yes."

My heart flipped. "You're asking me out on a date?"

"Yes. Isn't that what you wanted?"

Headache prickled behind my eyes and I pressed the heel of my hand against my forehead. I was so angry. It was more than just a slap, it was a betrayal. Sean was right. I should feel safe. I needed to feel safe.

"I don't feel safe, anymore."

"I know and I'm sorry. I messed up. Let me at least try to fix it." He was silent for a long moment. "You have all the power here, Redmond."

Fuck, that last statement broke me.

"Okay." I pulled my knees up to my chest and dropped my forehead onto them. "Fine. One date."

"Thank you, Redmond."

"This doesn't mean I forgive you."

"I know that. Cafe Dulce? Seven o'clock. If that works for you."

"Yeah. It's...fine."

"Okay. See you then."

I didn't know what else to say, so I just hung up.

* * *

I dressed much the same as I had the first time he took me to dinner. Black slacks and a button-up shirt, this one navy-blue. My hands shook so bad I could hardly button it and no matter how many times I told myself to calm down, I couldn't stop sweating. I'd made myself a deal. If things were to continue between Victor and me, it had to be on my terms. My rules. I'd given him my obedience too easily as if it were his due. From now on, it had to be earned. Anything less meant the brakes.

It sounded good in my head. I had a speech worked out and everything. It didn't make it any less scary.

"You look nice."

I jumped at Katie's voice from behind me. She leaned against the doorframe, twirling a lock of hair between her fingers. Her brows sat low over her eyes and her lower lip poked out a little, telling me she was still bruised from this morning.

"Thanks. I'm sorry I scared you last night."

She lowered her eyes and dug her big toe into the carpet.

"I'd just...had a weird day and all I wanted to do was forget it. I got way too drunk. I didn't want you to see me like that, so I spent the night at a friend's. I should have called you. I'm sorry."

"You have friends?" One of her brows twitched up and her head cocked to the side.

"Yes, I have friends." I stuck my tongue out at her and she laughed.

"You have another *business meeting?*"

"Actually, I have a date."

Her head snapped up and her eyes went wide as dinner plates. "What? With who? Oh my God, tell me everything."

She bounced her way toward me, and I had to grab her by the arms to settle her down. "Don't get too excited, kiddo. It may be nothing." But her excitement was contagious, and I had to bite my lip to keep from smiling as the knot in my stomach turned to butterflies. I steered her over to the bed and she plopped down on the edge, squirming like a kid on Christmas.

"Who is she? What's her name? Is she pretty?"

"Give me a break," I said, perching next to her. "Maybe I don't want to give up all my secrets just yet."

"But whyyyyyyyyyyyy?" she moaned, throwing herself back on the bed like a fainting damsel.

"Because if I give you any details, I'll come home to find you printing our wedding invitations."

"Fine." She sat up, her lips puckered into a tight pout. She went a little quiet, her toes digging into the carpet again. "You can talk to me about stuff, ya know," she said, "when you have a weird day."

Her words stuck a pin in my heart. I wanted to tell her everything. But now wasn't the time.

"Wait a minute." Her eyes narrowed and she peered into my face. "Is your date the *friend* you spent the night with?"

"Kaitlyn!"

She hopped off the bed and sped out of the room in a stream of giggles. I knew she was teasing but something jarred inside me like a car coming to a sudden stop. My head filled with the image of Sean curled up on the couch in nothing but his boxers, then sitting across from me at a dark table in Cafe Dulce. He'd wear a suit in a non-traditional color like royal-blue and it would set off the green in his eyes when he laughed, our feet bumping under the table as we drank shots of bad tequila.

*What the fuck?*

\* \* \*

I arrived at Cafe Dulce about ten minutes early and the same surly host led me to a corner booth toward the back of the dining room. The kind you have to slide into. That meant we would be sitting next to each other. *Next* to each other. Jesus Christ.

I pushed myself as far into the corner as I could go, immediately unrolling a napkin and dabbing at my hairline. The waiter asked for my drink order and I ordered a Cuba Libre—which is just a fancy name for rum and Coke—and drained half of it in one swallow. I ran my speech over in my head for the hundredth time, but all my practiced words went out the window when Victor walked through the door.

He was like oil on water, iridescent and beautiful. Light clung to him even in this dark place and he swam through it with a feline grace. He ran the lapel of his dark suit through his fingers as if appreciating the fine fabric. And his hands. God, his hands. I should have remembered the pain they caused, but all I could think of was their gentleness when he bathed me. Their sweetness when he held me. And their heat when he claimed me.

"Hello, Redmond."

I blinked and he appeared at the table as if he'd materialized from the ether. "H-hey."

I stiffened as he lowered himself into the seat. I expected him to slide right up next to me and something ached when he didn't.

"Have you ordered?"

I shook my head. "Just a drink."

"Would you like me to..."

"Sure. Fine. I wouldn't know what to get anyway."

The corners of his mouth twitched up and he waved down our waiter. He ordered just as before in perfect Italian, but his hands never stopped moving. Adjusting silverware, spinning stemware, toying with the edge of his napkin. Could it be he was nervous? Why on earth would he be nervous?

"Where did you learn Italian?" I asked.

He quirked his eyebrow at me. "Why?"

"Because I want to know," I said. "I don't know anything about you."

He smiled a little, his eyes softening. "I spent a year in Napoli before law school."

"Did you like it?"

"It was beautiful."

"That didn't answer the question."

"Yes, I liked it." He laughed and sipped at his drink. A dark-red wine I could smell from across the table. "Is that what this is going to be, Redmond? You quizzing me on my backstory?"

"Fuck you, all right. I don't know how to do this."

"Relaxing would be a good start."

I scoffed, my eyes darting around the busy dining room.

"They can't see us," he said, leaning across the table toward me. "That's why I reserved this table."

He pulled back as the waiter appeared to drop off our meals and a fresh round of drinks. I had some kind of pasta with what looked like mussels in a white sauce. Victor had a white fish fillet that smelled of rosemary. Everything so rich and decadent, it made me dizzy.

We ate in silence, or Victor did, taking small, delicate bites that drew my attention far too much to his mouth. I poked at my pasta, stirring it around in its thick sauce, my stomach too twisted to even take a bite.

"What do you want out of all this?" I asked.

Victor stopped eating, laying his silverware on the edge of his plate and folding his hands in front of him. "How do you want me to answer that, Redmond?"

"Truthfully."

He released a long breath through his nose and his eyes dropped to his plate. I tensed and averted my eyes as he slid down the bench seat toward me. My bruised cheek faced him and he lifted his fingers to touch it. They were so soft, so tender, it was hard to believe the same hand had put it there.

"I know what I don't want," he said, voice thick. "I don't want this to end."

"Then, you can't do that again. Ever."

He nodded. "I know."

"Taking care of me is more than just car engines and fancy dinners." I pivoted on my hip, forcing myself to face him even though my voice shook. "I have to trust you. To obey not because I fear the consequence, but because I know you want what's best for me. I am so lost. All the time."

I started to shake, and he wrapped my hand in his under the table. I clung to it like a lifeline. I wanted to climb into his lap and burrow into his chest like a child and hide from the world.

"I want to give you all of those things, Redmond." His voice cracked as he spoke and it startled me. "What angers me are not your failings, but mine."

He took a sharp breath and pulled away, settling back into his previous position. He ran his hands over his jacket and through his hair. The perfect, untouchable Victor returned, but his eyes were tired.

"I've thought about what you said last night," he said, plucking up his silverware and poking at his fish, "and I've come up with a compromise."

"A compromise?"

"I have a vacation house on Galveston Island."

"Okay..."

"It's far enough away from Black Creek where we could—"

"Are you asking me to go away with you?"

He put down his silverware again and folded his hands. *This is why he's nervous.* A laugh burst out of me before I could stop it and his eyes narrowed.

"What's funny?"

"Nothing. I'm just...surprised." I ran a hand over my face and scratched at the back of my neck. Logic told me this was a bad idea, going to another city with the man who hit me, but my heart did a happy little flip at the thought of time with him. Real time away from that sleazy club. Time meaning maybe I was worth more to him than just sex. I knew what I should do. I knew what Sean would tell me to do. But logic tended to take a back seat when it came to things Victor.

He arched an eyebrow at me. "So?"

"Okay," I said, shoving a wad of pasta into my mouth. He looked so hopeful, I just couldn't say no.

# Chapter 18

Victor and I planned our little getaway for the following weekend. Four days and three nights for us to start over, get to know each other in a different context away from the prying eyes of our neighbors. It wasn't exactly as I wanted, but it was close and it made me so nervous, I spent the whole week in a queasy haze. What if we didn't even like each other? What if it turned out sex was all we had? Or worse, what if he was exactly what Sean thought he was, and I ended up stuck on an island with an abusive asshole?

"You're awfully wound up for just a work trip," Katie said as she watched me repack my bag for the hundredth time. She lay crosswise across the end of my bed, chin resting in her hands and feet kicking in the air. I'd told her Bo was sending me to Houston to talk to a supplier, the same lie I told Sean, and the weight of it sat like a stone on my chest.

"This is my one chance to get in good with Bo. I just don't want to screw it up, is all. And I'm worried about leaving you here alone."

That part was true. I hadn't left her longer than overnight since she'd come to live with me and my mind raced with all the things that could go wrong. Skipping school to throw a house party. Car accidents. Kitchen fires.

She rolled her eyes at me. "Please, Red. I'm not thirteen anymore. I can take care of myself."

"Promise me, if you need anything, you'll call your mother."

She wrinkled her nose and turned her face away.

"Katie, I'm serious," I said, pinching her ear to get her attention. "She can get here faster than I can if something happens."

"Fiiiiiine." She flopped over on her side with a pout. "Just promise me you'll at least try to have some fun while you're gone."

"Promise." The corners of my mouth lifted, and I had to swallow a burst of butterflies. "I leave early in the morning. You gonna be up to see me off?"

"Not a chance."

I laughed. "Okay. Well, it's late. I gotta get some sleep."

She rolled onto her back and wiggled her toes at the ceiling.

"Katie—"

"Oh! Right. Okay." She slid off the bed, popped up beside me, and planted a kiss on my temple. "Love you, brother."

"You too, kiddo."

She skipped out of the room and closed the door behind her. I waited until I heard her door slam down the hall before crossing the room to my dresser. I pulled open my underwear drawer and reached all the way to the back, where I wrapped my hand around the now familiar leather collar. Despite all my tall talk, I didn't feel right without it. This trip wasn't about change but evolution. I still liked being owned, being cared for. I still wanted to be his dog. But I wanted a piece of him too. Something he was not quite as eager to give up.

My phone vibrated on the nightstand just as I zipped up my bag. A text message from Sean.

*Have a good trip and leave some hotties for me <3*

I laughed and started typing out a return text but hit the call button instead.

"You know, it's more likely to be a bunch of rednecks with beer bellies, right?" I said when the call connected. We didn't even bother with greetings anymore.

"Oh, I dunno," he purred. "A bunch of burly, greased-up mechanics..."

I dropped down onto the bed, back against the headboard. "I didn't realize that was your thing."

"Neither did I." A beat of silence. "I wish I could go with you. I could use a break from this town."

"I thought you were gonna say you could use a burly mechanic."

"That too." He laughed. "I think I might miss you a little bit while you're gone."

"Me too." It surprised me how much I meant it. Ever since my coming out breakdown, something had shifted in our relationship. Subtle, but profound. I could be myself, my real self, with him more than anyone. Even Victor. I laughed easier, breathed easier, like a snake finally shedding a skin that was too tight.

"When do you leave tomorrow?"

"W—I want to be on the road by seven." God, I hated lying to him.

"Ouch. You better get some sleep. Let me know when you get there?"

My whole body warmed. I'd never had somebody to worry over me, to miss me when I was gone. I mean, besides Katie.

"Okay." I leaned my head back on the headboard and closed my eyes. "See you in a couple days."

"See you."

\* \* \*

Since everyone I knew thought I was driving alone to Houston, Victor and I met at the plantation. I pulled my truck into the nearly empty driveway and I parked around a hidden bend. Victor's BMW rolled up a minute later, signaling me with a quick beep of his horn. He popped the trunk without getting out and I tossed my bag inside before jumping into the passenger seat.

"Good morning, Redmond."

I did a double take as the door slammed closed. My usual prim and pressed Victor had been replaced with someone from an Abercrombie catalogue. He wore loose-fitting distressed denim that showed hints of skin over his knees and a T-shirt made from some soft material that made me want to drag my hands over his chest. His hair was pulled into a low ponytail and dark shades perched on the top of his head.

"What?"

"Nothing," I said, shaking my head. "It's just...you look so different."

"I don't live in a suit, Redmond," he said, brows lowering.

"I mean, I like it." I laid my hand over his on the gear shift and he flinched a little. His fingers curled just enough to let me in, and he inhaled sharply as if the gesture disarmed him. I liked that too.

He cleared his throat and pulled his hand out of mine to rest on the steering wheel. "Ready to go?"

I relaxed back into my seat. "Yessir."

We slid out onto the highway and before I knew it, the East Texas flatland was whipping past my window to the tune of light jazz. Victor tapped his fingers on the steering wheel and his head bobbed to the beat. A lock of hair fell loose from his ponytail and fluttered against his cheek.

A strange feeling started beneath my skin. Not the sharp, electric arousal I was used to with him, but a low frequency hum that made my heart pump a little harder. I'd always seen him as a sculpture of himself, beautiful but also cold and ultimately untouchable.

But this was different. Like a fairy tale, the statue had been magicked to life and was now soft and warm and so close.

I had to touch him. I leaned forward, brushing my fingers along his cheekbone as I caught that lock of hair and tucked it behind his ear. The corners of his mouth lifted as he caught my hand in his and brought my knuckles to his lips. I could have wept from the sweetness of it.

There it was. That feeling that might be love.

"What brings a person like you to Black Creek?"

"What do you mean?" he asked, dropping our entwined hands into his lap.

"I mean, you're obviously not from there."

"Obviously?" He quirked an eyebrow in my direction.

"You know what I mean. You're not like everyone else. You're... I don't know...cultured. Like old money cultured."

"There's not old money in Black Creek?"

"Sure there is, but it's all in cattle or oil—"

"Or lumber."

I flinched at the reference to the Delaneys. "Yeah. Blue collar at its core. You're different."

"You're right," he said with a soft laugh. "I'm from New Hampshire originally. My family made their money in real estate, though it's mostly just stocks now."

"Why did you leave?"

He released a long breath. "Wealthy families there are complicated. Basically aristocracy. I grew up knowing my whole life was already laid out for me. Go to the best school. The obligatory year abroad. Get the advanced degree and a fancy job. Get married."

"They didn't know..."

"They knew." His words had an edge to them, and his hand tightened around mine. "It didn't matter. Appearance is everything. Marry a girl from a good family. Check all the boxes. Indulge your tastes with discretion."

"Well, if you wanted to be gay in the open, you picked a strange place—"

"It wasn't even about that," he said. "It was about living a life that was mine. My choices, my...shame."

My chest ached. I wanted to tell him not to be ashamed of who he was, but it rang hollow.

"My father knew." I swallowed hard against the stone in my throat. "When I was fifteen, he found a magazine hidden under my mattress. I came home from school one day and he was there sitting on my bed with it rolled up tight in his fist. He didn't say anything, he just started hitting me with it. It's amazing how much that hurts."

A heavy silence fell over us. It struck me then we weren't so different, Victor and I. Both of us shaped by the pain of our past. We were told what we were was wrong, and we believed it. So, we shoved the truth down into some deep, dark place where we couldn't hurt anyone but ourselves. But lately, that feeling had been slipping away. I had Victor to thank for that, at least in part. His control had cracked me open and shown me the part of myself I was afraid of. Turns out I wasn't that bad.

"Thank you," I said, voice thick with unexpected emotion.

"For what?"

"For taking such good care of me."

\* \* \*

We stopped in Pearland for a long, leisurely meal before jumping onto I-45 and crossing the bridge to Galveston Island. The mid-afternoon sun skipped off the still waters of the bay, making every-thing gold. I rolled down the window and breathed in the ocean air. I caught Victor's eye before leaning my head out and letting my tongue loll, face and hair buffeted by the wind. He laughed, deep and loud, and that alone was worth the trip.

We drove down a winding road between beaches and resort hotels to a quiet, sprawling neighborhood. His house was, of course, at the back edge, far from any neighbors and right on the beach. A simple but picturesque beach house, the kind you see on the cover of magazines, sat framed by ocean and sky. White siding and pale-blue trim made it fade into the landscape as if it were born from it.

Victor popped the trunk and then tossed me the keys. "Take your shoes off before you go in."

I nodded and headed up a set of wooden stairs to the front porch while Victor unloaded our bags. The door swung open with a groan, and I gasped at the beauty of the place. It wasn't big, maybe a thousand square feet, with a wide-open floor plan. The entire back wall was made up of floor-to-ceiling windows facing the beach and a long, weather-beaten pier. I expected something sleek and ultra-modern, but the place was surprisingly rustic with natural wood furniture and textured concrete floors.

"I had the housekeepers air the place out for us," Victor said from behind me as he pushed through the door and dropped our bags in the entryway, "but it's a constant battle with the sand here, so—"

As soon as his hands were empty, I threw myself into them, knocking him back into the wall. He made a small sound of surprise when I wrapped my arms around his neck and crushed my lips to his.

"What was that for?" he asked when after I released him.

"Sorry, I just..." My heart skipped over the inside of my ribcage and I laughed. "I've been wanting to do that since we left Black Creek."

He smiled and kissed me again. Gentle at first, then more force-ful, greedy, and I let him take all he wanted of me. That low hum I'd been feeling all day turned into a throbbing ache as he pulled me tight against him.

As always, he pulled back too soon, leaving me weak and

breathless. "Did you bring it?" he asked against my lips. I nodded. "Give it to me."

Knees like Jell-O, I dropped down to the floor next to my bag and yanked it open. The collar lay coiled inside my boots and I pulled it out. The leather heated in my hand as if it knew what was to come, as if it, too, burned with anticipation.

Without standing, I pivoted on my hip to face Victor. He still leaned back against the wall, pupils dilated, cheeks slightly pink, lips swollen. He straightened when I held the collar out to him, my head lowered in submission.

"Good boy," he said in a husky voice. He took the collar in one hand, running the other through my hair. I held my breath, expecting him to put it on me, but instead he walked past me and into the kitchen. I didn't move until I heard the refrigerator open.

I scrambled to my feet and found him at the kitchen island, pouring two glasses of white wine. He'd looped the collar through his belt, and it bounced against his hip as he moved, a not-so-subtle reminder of who was in charge. He'd given me a little control with this trip, the conversation in the car, that kiss. Now, he was taking it back.

"We should go for a walk." He pushed one glass toward me before lifting the other to his lips. The wine was sweet and so cold it hurt. "It's a beautiful day to be on the beach. There's a general store about a half mile down. We're stocked with the basics here, but..."

He followed my eye line down to his hip, lips curling in a soundless laugh. He came around to my side of the island and cupped my chin in his hand, forcing my eyes up.

"There's plenty of time for that, Redmond."

I took a shaky breath and nodded. I jumped when my phone vibrated in my pocket. I cleared my throat and took a step back before pulling it out and checking the screen.

Sean.

"It's my sister," I said, guilt burning through me like hot lead. I gestured toward the back door. "I'm just going to..."

Victor shrugged and turned his attention back to his wine as I ducked around him and out the sliding glass doors onto the back porch. A charcoal grill sat tucked in the corner next to a wrought iron dinette and I made a mental note to grab a couple of steaks from the store.

"Did you make it alive? I was about to send out a search party," Sean said as soon as I answered.

"Sorry, I got kind of tied up."

"You forgot."

"Yeah, I forgot."

He laughed. "How's the accommodations?"

"Good, actually," I said. "You should see the view."

"Show me."

I glanced over my shoulder into the house. Victor still stood at the island, back half turned to me while sipping his wine. I switched my phone to camera mode and took a quick shot of the beach.

"Wow," Sean said.

"I know, right."

"If you don't fish off that pier, you're dead to me."

I spun around at the sound of rapping on the window behind me. Victor, his wineglass now empty, knocked on the glass with his knuckles, lifting his eyebrows in a gesture of impatience.

"I've gotta go. I'll catch up with you later."

"Okay. Have fun."

I clicked off, fired off a quick text to Katie—couldn't have her calling and blowing my cover—and ducked back inside. Victor met me with my half-finished glass of wine in one hand and my shoes in the other.

"Everything okay?"

"Yeah, she just wanted to make sure I made it safe."

He nodded and tapped the rim of my glass. I finished the remains of my wine in one swallow and he took it back with a smile of approval. After depositing the glass on the counter, he drifted past me and out of the back door, leaving my shoes positioned neatly at the bottom of the steps leading to the beach. He signaled me with a sharp whistle, and I snapped to attention.

He had me so well trained.

He was right, the walk was beautiful. The beach was deserted, the neighborhood just far enough away to pretend it wasn't there and we were the only people alive. I took my shoes off and walked in the surf, the gentle push and pull of the ocean tugging at my ankles. I lifted my face to the sun, and it warmed me to my bones.

It was about a ten-minute walk to the general store. I grabbed a couple of steaks and a bag of charcoal while Victor complained about the wine selection. He bought a couple of bottles anyway. He insisted on carrying the entire load on the way back, and the whole thing was so domestic, I had to bite my cheek to keep from laughing.

When we got back to the house, I fired up the grill and the steaks were done just in time to watch the sunset from the back porch. We pulled our chairs close together, and I leaned on his shoulder while the sky burst into flame. Yellows and oranges and deep reds burned the air into star-sprinkled black, the sky so close you could almost touch it.

"God, I could sit out here forever," I said. We had polished off another bottle of wine and that combined with the sound of the ocean made me drowsy and light.

"And I could eat your steaks every night," he said with a rumbling laugh. "They were perfect."

A burst of warmth colored my cheeks and I pushed my nose into the crook of his neck. He had let his hair loose and the salt air lent it a spiciness that made my skin tingle. "I think I may be a little drunk."

"Is that so?" I hummed in affirmation and when he planted a kiss on my forehead, I felt him smile. "I'll clear the table then."

I groaned in protest as he gathered up the dishes and disappeared into the house, leaving me alone. I let my head fall back, closed my eyes, and imagined a world where we could live like this. Two people sitting on the porch watching the sunset and being together without worrying about who would see, who would judge. It didn't seem so out of reach suddenly and my heart swelled with profound gratitude.

Reality snapped back around me at the familiar sensation of leather against my neck. My fingers curled around the arms of the chair, but I didn't move, didn't open my eyes. My breathing came in short, ragged gasps as Victor's fingers brushed over my skin and secured the buckle.

"Come inside, Redmond."

Every nerve ending popped to life in an electric cascade at his simple command. His hands disappeared, followed by the hiss of a sliding door. Funny, I hadn't heard him come out. I blinked my eyes open and pivoted in my chair just enough to see him standing next to it, expression cold, head high. He would only wait so long.

I slid out of the chair onto my hands and knees. His eyebrows lifted with smug approval and he went inside ahead of me. I followed at his heels, head low, one eye trained on him. He stopped in the center of the open living area and turned his eyes back on me.

He signaled me to my feet with a snap of his fingers. "You're my dog, aren't you, Redmond?" he asked, hooking a finger under my collar and pulling me closer.

"Yessir." Fuck, I was already hard.

"You're a good dog who obeys his Master." His lips were so close they brushed against mine.

"Yessir."

"Good." He released my collar and stepped back, hands folded behind his back. "Clothes off."

Dizzy from the wine and heart pounding in my ears, I struggled out of my clothes and left them draped over the back of the couch. Victor's eyes left a trail of sparks as they raked over my exposed flesh and swollen cock, but he remained composed.

"Sit."

I dropped to my haunches.

"Stay."

I swallowed a groan as he turned his back on me and disappeared down the hall to the bedroom. I knew this was coming, the inevitable power play, and it tugged hard at my arousal. Every second he made me wait dragged on for hours, and I was hunched and trembling by the time he returned. He had changed his clothes, and now wore a fresh T-shirt and a pair of loose-fitting gym shorts and carried a drawstring bag. He dropped into the sofa, setting the bag on the table beside him with a heavy sound.

He spent a moment getting comfortable, arranging throw pillows and sinking himself into the cushions, and I thought I would combust before he finally patted his knee. I scrambled across the concrete floor and stopped at his feet. He leaned forward and ran a hand through my hair.

"My, you are anxious today, aren't you, Redmond?" he cooed with a soft smile. I whined and leaned into his hand. His expression hardened as he hooked a finger in my collar again and pulled me up closer between his knees. "Since you've been such a good boy, I'll let you come whenever you want. But don't touch yourself unless I tell you. Don't touch me unless I tell you. And no matter what, you're not done until I'm finished with you. Understand?"

"Y-yessir."

"Good." He released me and relaxed back into the sofa. His posture was calm, but his track shorts did nothing to hide his growing bulge. "Give me your hand, Redmond."

My hand shook as I lifted it toward him. I expected him to put it on his cock, but he lifted it to his face, pulling me up onto my knees to cover the distance. He pressed his nose into my palm and took a deep, ragged breath.

"You smell like your steaks," he said. I bit back a moan as he ran his tongue from my wrist to the end of my ring finger. "Taste like them too."

He continued tasting my skin, trailing open-mouthed kisses along the edge of my palm and down my forearm that sent electric shocks through my pelvis. The position had me practically in his lap, my hips pressed against the couch, and the pressure was unbearable.

*Come whenever you want.*

Fuck, I wanted to come right now.

*Don't touch yourself.*

I adjusted my weight on my knees and, keeping a careful eye on Victor's reaction, rolled my hips against the couch. A choked sound like a sob escaped me as the rough fabric scraped across my skin. Victor watched out of the corner of his eye, a smile curling his lips as he sucked one of my fingers into his mouth.

He took them so deep I felt the back of his throat on my fingertips and my bones vibrated as I imagined his pretty lips wrapped around something else. He hooked one leg around me, his foot sliding up the back of my thigh and pressing me even tighter against the couch. The friction against my cock almost painful, the need to come even more so. I clutched at the pillows beside Victor with my free hand and he laughed darkly.

"You want it so bad, you'll hump the couch. What a horny bitch you are."

"Please, sir. Please, please..." The words came out slurred, cut by sobs. I felt transported, my body alive with pleasure and humiliation just as it had been on our first night together when I'd humped his leg like a lush.

"I told you, Redmond. You don't need my permission—"

My body spasmed and back arched as the cork popped on my arousal. Rainbow sparks flashed behind my eyes as my release pulsed against the couch and splashed to the floor. I slumped against Victor's leg as waves of euphoria surged through me.

"That's a good boy, Redmond," he said, voice husky. He slid his hand up and down the line of my spine as my body cooled. I hadn't realized how pent up I was, how needy I was for his control.

That's what this was all about, wasn't it? For both of us. He wanted to subjugate me, turn me into his obedient lapdog, and I wanted to see the heat in his eyes as his restraint shattered. Only when you are broken can you be set free.

I nuzzled into his thigh, eyes pinned to the tent just inches from my nose. He hooked his thumb in his waistband and pulled it down, allowing his erection to bob free. I lifted my head, licked my lips, and whined.

"You want a taste?" He ran his hand in a languid manner up and down his shaft, a pearl of fluid on his head showing he was more worked up than he let on. I nodded my head and wiggled my body like a dog begging for a treat. "Okay, Redmond. Just a taste."

I leaned forward and dragged my tongue over the entire length of him. He sucked in a breath and shuddered. He still held my hand and his grip tightened as I peppered the head with tiny licks.

"That's enough, Redmond." His voice was breathy, tremulous. He hooked his free hand in my collar and gave it a tug. "Come up here with me."

Body still loose from my recent orgasm, I allowed him to pull me up into his lap. I settled with his hips between my knees, his cock pressed against the cleft of my ass. Deep-red splotches colored his cheeks as he pressed our chests together and pinned both my wrists against my lower back.

Trapped. Unable to move unless he moved me. The motor

inside me revved up again as he held me there motionless, studying me with hazy eyes.

He leaned forward and placed the smallest of kisses against the corner of my mouth. Just a grazing of lips and teeth. He pushed his hips up while applying pressure to my lower back, forcing my body to roll against his. Another nip at my lips, another roll. I went all but limp to his control, a buzz starting in my head as his chest heaved against mine.

"Can you get hard for me again, Redmond?" he whispered against my skin.

"Yessir." I was halfway there already.

He hummed and claimed my lips again, harder this time, his tongue forcing its way between my teeth. It was like a drug, his tongue, obliterating all coherent thought and reducing me to nothing but a mass of needy moans. His hips thrust upward again, and I screamed into his mouth as his cock brushed against my hole.

"You want me inside you, don't you?" he asked with my bottom lip between his teeth. I responded in garbled syllables, arching my back to increase the contact. "Or would you rather be inside me?"

My engine screamed as if he'd just floored the gas. "Oh, God, Jesus, fuck, yes, please."

"I want to come with you inside me, Redmond." His voice shook and his thighs trembled beneath mine. "Get hard for me."

I was so hard I could cut glass and I pressed it against his belly as he thrust up against me. His breathing went jagged, laced with moans, and I feared he was already too far gone. But then, he canted his hips and tossed me onto my back on the couch. He pinned my wrists over my head and just hovered over me, panting, sweat beading across his brow.

*Trust me, Victor. Come undone for me.*

"Stay," he said finally, releasing my wrists and rocking back upright. I didn't move, eyes tracking him as he stood up. His expression had gone hard again, and he snatched up the drawstring bag he'd brought from the bedroom. He pulled out a box of condoms and a bottle of lube. Fuck, this was really happening.

I flinched as if he'd branded me when he pulled a condom off the strip and dropped it on my chest. He set the lube bottle down next to the couch before peeling off his shirt and kicking out of his shorts.

"Fuck, you're beautiful," I groaned. His eyes softened a bit, and he positioned himself over me again, my hips between his knees, and his long body stretched out above me.

He plucked up the condom and held it up to my lips. "You might be my best dog yet, Redmond."

I smiled and, with a growl, caught the wrapper between my teeth and tore it open. My hips twitched with anticipation as he rolled the condom out over me and coated me with lube. He drizzled it over his own fingers and reached behind him, his eyes pinching shut as he hastily prepped himself.

This was it. My mind wound back to that first shameful fantasy I'd had in his car. This was what I'd wanted, what I'd dreamed of.

He lowered himself over me achingly slowly and we moaned in unison. My heart pounded and I felt every beat in my cock. His too. I gripped the pillows over my head so hard I would swear I'd ripped them open. The muscles of my abdomen flexed and coiled against the pressure building in my pelvis.

Victor rocked his hips, sending a jolt of electricity through me, and I panicked. I tried to follow his rules, I tried, but my hands flew to his thighs as if on their own. He growled and grabbed my wrists, forcing them back up over my head and pinning me with an icy glare.

"I'm sorry, I'm sorry," I mumbled, my head thrashing back and forth in an effort to escape. "Don't move. If you move, I'm gonna come, and then I can't—"

"Shhhh." Victor bent low over me and brushed his lips over mine. "Trust me. I've got you."

He kissed me again, so soft and sweet my insides glowed. My body relaxed and he interlaced his fingers with mine as he started to move. We sighed against each other's lips, and his slow rhythm accelerated. I thrust up into him, reaching for the sweet spot that would make him come apart.

"Ah, fuck, touch me, Redmond," he cried, pulling one of my hands between us. I stroked him hard as my hips stuttered, biting the inside of my cheek until it bled. His back arched and he threw his head back as he came. His body spasmed around me, pulling me over the edge with him, and my overheated engine exploded in a burst of steam.

For a long time, neither of us moved, the only sound our trembling breaths. Victor's hair fell around his face like a curtain. I ached to see him. Despite his rules, I slipped my hand out of his grip and pushed it back. He didn't stop me. Instead, he leaned into me and when his eyes lifted to mine, they were so open it nearly brought me to tears.

# Chapter 19

After we caught our breath, we stumbled into the bathroom and into a garden tub where we lay back to chest, feet tangled up together, until the water went cold. When we finally made it to the bed, I thought he might make me sleep on the floor or curled up at his feet, but he pulled me right up against him, and I fell asleep with his heartbeat in my ear.

I don't think I'd ever slept so well.

The next morning, I woke before he did. His lay with his back to me and his hair fanned out on the pillow behind him. I couldn't help myself. I buried my nose in it, breathing in the sweet scent of him. I couldn't remember the last time I'd woken up beside somebody without at least a trace of shame, but here, I felt only joy. I remembered that openness in his eyes and my heart fluttered.

Did he feel it too?

I kissed his shoulder, but he didn't stir, so I decided to let him sleep. I slipped out of bed and into a living room bathed in morning light. My face burned when I spotted our mess from the night before. It appeared so debauched in the sober light of day, nothing like the soul-cracking event it was.

While hunting through closets in search of cleaning supplies, I stumbled upon a fishing rod propped in a corner. It looked fancy—top of the line, I'm sure—but it still had the tags on. A smile tugged at my lips as I remembered my conversation with Sean the day before. I snatched it up along with a package of foie gras I found in the fridge and headed out in flip-flops and a robe to the pier.

I tried to remember everything Sean taught me as I threaded the line through the pole and baited my hook. I leaned the pole against the railing and settled into a rusted folding chair. The sun had already warmed the air to glowing and it melted into my skin. I pulled out my phone and snapped a photo of the view, my pole in the foreground, and sent it to Sean. I received a response a few seconds later. *I kind of hate you right now* followed by a frowning emoji with a green face.

I hovered my finger over the call button and a needle of guilt pierced my happy bubble. I wanted to call him. Wanted to tell him all about my night with Victor so we could gush like a couple of girlfriends. But I'd created a cocoon of lies around our relationship and instead of keeping us safe, it suffocated us.

A sharp whistle snapped my attention back to the house. Victor stood at the back door in his boxers, a cup of coffee in his hand. "Shit," I muttered as I retrieved my line and scrambled back down the pier. He was already inside by the time I got back, perched on a stool at the kitchen island sipping coffee and reading a paper. He didn't look up when I walked in.

"Morning."

His eyes cut to me and then back down to his paper. My stomach twisted into a knot as I crossed to the kitchen. The smell of coffee filled the air, and I filled a mug from a French press on the counter. I sat next to him and watched his fingers flick through the pages over the rim of my cup.

"Am I in trouble?" I asked when the silence had become too heavy to bear.

"Why would you be in trouble, Redmond?"

"I'm sorry. You just looked so...I didn't want to wake you."

He dropped his paper with a sigh and laid a hand on my forearm. "You're not in trouble. Though I had hoped to wake up with you next to me, this morning."

"I—"

He pressed his fingertips to my lips. "No more apologizing." He ran the pad of his thumb over my lower lip and then leaned forward and kissed me. The knot in my stomach unwound, releasing a whole flock of butterflies.

Victor stood from the island and started to make us breakfast, French toast with lots of cinnamon that made the whole house smell like Christmas. I offered to help, but he shooed me away, so I resigned myself to enjoying the view. The way the muscles of his back worked under his skin made me hungrier than the food.

He loaded the toast up all on one plate and set it between us on the island. Instead of handing me a fork, he fed me bite by bite as we talked plans for the day. He had everything laid out, of course. Shopping on The Strand, lunch at a resort restaurant, drinks at a bar downtown. I just nodded along, caught in his river, happy to go wherever it took me.

And it took me to grand places. As we walked down the quaint streets filled with the happy bustle of tourists, close together, shoulders touching, I felt a peace I didn't know existed. Victor watched over me as I peered into shop windows and laughed at the kitschy wares, a soft smile warming his face. He bought a wood carving of a Great Dane which he presented to me over ice cream at a roadside cafe, leaving me red-faced and squirming.

It was perfect and by the time we were ready for drinks, my feet hardly touched the ground. As we wandered toward the downtown bar district, I took a chance and slipped my hand into his. My happy bubble lost some air when Victor pulled away. Not a total rejection—he gave me a little squeeze before tucking his hand into his pocket—but it stung, nonetheless. He couldn't let go of his shame even here with no one to see us save faceless tourists, and my fragile fantasy took quite the knock.

On our way toward a posh whiskey bar on the far end of the street, we passed a pair of men standing very close together in front of a club emitting a heavy bass beat. One had his fingers hooked in the other's hip pocket and both wore the dizzy smiles of attraction. The scene stirred something inside me, and I grabbed Victor's arm.

"Look," I said under my breath, pointing with my eyes toward the two men. Victor glanced their way and then arched his eyebrow at me as if to say, *What's your point?* More men filtered in and out of the bar behind them, letting out bursts of laughter and synthesized music. "Do you think it's a gay bar?"

"I think it's a noise violation," he said with a sour face.

"I want to go in."

"No." His brows lowered over his eyes, and he started back down the street.

I didn't move. "Please, Victor."

"I said no, Redmond."

A fire ignited in my gut. "What's the point of being here if you're embarrassed to be with me?"

He stopped, taking a long breath before turning back to face me. "It's just a bar, Redmond."

"It's a safe place." I halved the distance between us, and his posture stiffened. "Please."

He glanced back up at the bar, lips pursed, a little wrinkle forming over the bridge of his nose. "Is it that important to you?"

"Yes."

He sighed, one corner of his mouth twitching upward as he gestured for me to lead the way. I wanted to kiss him but decided not to press my luck. Instead, I practically skipped up the street with Victor trailing behind me. The two men I'd seen had moved on by the time we reached the club, and the entrance was deserted save for a burly security guy with a prominent lisp. He checked our

IDs and made a big show of checking Victor out before holding the door open for us.

Inside was a wash of sensory information that left me temporarily blinded. First was music, loud and throbbing, the kind you felt deep in your bones. Next was heat. A press of bodies swarmed within a pool of light like anxious moths, clouding the air with sweat and musk. My head reeled with it, the carnal nature of it, with an energy not unlike that sex den back home only hidden in subtext. Bodies writhed together on a small dance floor in an imitation of acts to come, and I had to grasp Victor's arm to keep my balance.

"Look at this place," I gasped.

"Yes, look at it," he said with a curl of his lip. He braced one hand against the bar as a crowd of men passed and then pulled it back with a grimace and wiped it with a handkerchief.

I laughed, thrilled by seeing Victor so out of his element. I pushed up to the bar, and at least half a dozen men gave me a once-over, making my heart race. It was glorious. Not just the attention, but the openness, the freedom. A hundred men just like me dancing and laughing and touching and none of them afraid or ashamed because there was nothing wrong with us.

I ordered a white wine for Victor and a whiskey Coke for myself. Victor looked no more comfortable than when I had left him, and he eyed the wineglass with suspicion when I pushed it into his hand.

"Don't be such a snob for once. Relax." I stepped up against him, pressing my chest right up against his and laying my free hand on his hip. The muscles of his jaw jumped, but he didn't push me away. His eyes darted around the room and I gave him a little tug. "If anyone sees us together here, it means they're here too."

His eyes dropped back down to mine, the hardness leaking away as he gave in. He slipped his arm around me, slowly, tentatively, as if I were a trap that would spring the moment he showed any affection. I drained my drink in one great swallow and dropped the glass on a nearby table before wrapping myself fully around him and swaying to the beat.

For a moment, I wondered what they put in those drinks, but it wasn't the booze making me drunk. I slid my hands up Victor's chest, along the line of his neck, and rested them against his jaw. I wanted this. For him, for me, for Sean back in Black Creek who could hardly leave his house. For every queer kid afraid to tell his family or fall in love.

"Kiss me," I said against his cheek, my voice choked with unexpected emotion.

His arm tightened around me. "No."

"Please." I lined my face up to his, just millimeters away as if the distance was the problem.

"People will see—"

"Let them see. Show them I'm yours." My voice hitched, and my hands balled in his hair. "Please, Victor, I need this."

"Why?" His hands gripped my shoulders, holding me in place.

"So, I can feel normal for once in my goddamn life." Tears sprang to my eyes and I squeezed them closed to keep them from falling. His grip tightened and for a brief shining moment my heart leaped with the hope he would pull me closer only to crash at my feet when he pushed me away.

"You know I would give you anything," he said, his voice so soft, I hardly heard it over the music. My heart broke. He'd given me the push I needed, and I'd ended up in a place he couldn't follow. Everything was suddenly too loud, too bright, too much. Eyes on the floor, I pulled out of his grip and was swept up by the crowd. Heart pounding, head reeling, I fought against the current of sweaty bodies and out into the humid night air.

I made it about half a block before collapsing against a lamp-post. The streets had mostly cleared, giving the impression of total isolation. I sucked in deep breaths, the air thick as sea water.

Victor's aura burned hot against my back, but I didn't turn around. I couldn't turn around.

"I'm sorry, Redmond."

"I've been so happy these past two days," I said, "but we can't ever have this, can we? Not really."

I pulled myself up straight and turned to face him. He looked battered. Pain, sadness, regret twitched across his face and his shoulders sagged with the weight. His careful control was gone, and I'd taken it from him.

"I'm just so fucking tired, Victor. Tired of believing what I feel for you is something to be ashamed of."

"You think I'm ashamed of you?"

"No. I think you're ashamed of yourself."

He sucked in a sharp breath and his eyes pinched. He opened his mouth to speak, but the words got stuck. His weight shifted as if to step toward me, but that got stuck too.

"It's not your fault," I said. "Of course, you believe it. But it's not true, Victor. There's nothing wrong with us. It's taken me so long to realize that and maybe one day you'll realize that, too, but I can't—" A sob scrambled up my throat, and I bit down on it.

"You can't wait for me," he finished for me, his voice ragged. I shook my head. "This is the brakes, isn't it?"

I nodded and drifted as close to him as his comfort would allow. "I'll always be grateful for you."

# Chapter 20

I slept on the couch that night despite Victor's protests. Sleeping next to him didn't feel right under the circumstances. So, I took a bottle of wine from the fridge and sat out on the pier. Out there, surrounded by water the same black as the sky, I let the tears flow. I wasn't angry at Victor. Two days ago, I might have even reacted the same way. But I was scared. I'd crossed a line within myself and stood firmly in the unknown. I couldn't go back, didn't want to go back, but facing it alone felt like driving toward a wall with no airbags.

I pulled my phone out of my pocket and scrolled through the short contact list in search of a lifeline. I desperately wanted to talk to Sean, but telling him about this would be admitting I'd lied yet again, so like a coward I flicked past his name and landed on Katie's instead.

The phone rang twice before she answered with a groggy, "Hello?"

"Hey, kiddo."

"Red? Are you okay? God, what time is it?"

"Late."

"I have school tomorrow, ya know."

"Sorry. I just...missed you." My voice cracked and I pinched the bridge of my nose to keep the tears from starting up again. "I had a really weird day."

A beat. "You wanna talk about it?"

"Yeah," I said with a sigh. "But when I get home, okay? Why don't you tell me about your weekend?"

"Oh, last night I threw the most epic party," she said, a smile in her voice. "Like half the school turned up. We had a keg in the bathtub and kids were having sex right on the living room floor. It was iconic."

"You better be fucking with me."

"Of course, I am."

We laughed and a little of the weight lifted. The world hadn't changed so much after all.

"It's weird not having you here," she said. "I guess I miss you too."

"Gee, thanks."

"You sure you're okay?"

"Yeah, I'm fine. I'll see you tomorrow, okay? Love you, kiddo."

"Love you, too, brother."

* * *

The sun was high when I finally woke. I'd slept the sleep of the terminally exhausted, deep and dreamless. My face was sticky and eyes raw, and I peeled them open with great effort. The smell of coffee nudged at my nose, meaning Victor was already awake. I lay on my back and stared at the ceiling, surprisingly calm. I had agreed to this weekend in the hope something would change and of course, it had. Maybe not in exactly the way I wanted. Still, I felt some relief. I knew who I was. More importantly, I had accepted it, embraced it, and I was no longer willing to compromise even if it meant taking losses. None were so great as the loss of myself.

Victor sat at the kitchen island and his eyes flicked toward me as I pulled myself upright. Part of me expected him to be wounded, but he was as composed as ever. He'd already showered and dressed in khaki slacks and a white button-up shirt, sleeves rolled up his forearms and tail out. He wore his hair in a high ponytail that accentuated his sharp features and made him look like a cartoon samurai. Both our bags were packed and stacked neatly by the door.

"What time is it?"

"Nearly ten," he answered, eyes cutting back down to his paper.

"You could have woken me."

"What would be the point of that, Redmond?"

I flinched despite his even tone. "Have you eaten—"

"Yes."

"Okay." I sighed and made my way to the kitchen. No leftovers, no covered plates, only a single small pan drying on a rack. He'd cooked only for himself. He was no longer taking care of me.

"Make it fast. We should get on the road."

"Yessir," I muttered under my breath as I searched the pantry. I found a box of cherry Pop-Tarts and threw a couple in the toaster. I leaned on the counter as I waited for them to heat and studied Victor's back. "Should we talk?"

He didn't turn. "About what, Redmond?"

"About last night."

"Were you expecting me to have some sort of epiphany?"

"No," I said. "Some feelings, maybe."

His shoulders dropped a little, but he didn't respond. My phone chimed from the living room and I crossed past him to get it.

"You have to come home," Katie's panicked voice barked through the receiver.

"Calm down. What happened?"

"I got in trouble at school," she said, and her words wobbled. "I've been suspended for the day."

"Goddammit, Katie—"

"It wasn't my fault!"

"It never is, is it?"

"You have to come get me."

"Call that driver of yours. Get him to take you home."

"I tried," she said. "The school will only release me to a parent or guardian."

My heart froze. "I'm at least four hours away. What do you expect me to do?"

"Just get here, okay?" Her voice broke. "They're gonna call Dad."

A muffled, authoritative voice appeared in the background and the line clicked off. My stomach dropped and my skin went cold. If the school called the Colonel, one of two things would happen: he would ignore the call, believing his troubled daughter wasn't worth his time, or he would take her away from me, citing her behavior as yet another of my many failures.

"We have to go."

Victor looked up, brows low over his eyes. "What's wrong?"

"It's my sister. I have to get home, now." My hands shook and my throat tightened around the words.

"Is she okay?" He popped up out of his chair and moved toward me.

"My father...shit, they'll call the Colonel." My legs gave out and I fell into the couch, elbows on knees and the heels of my hands pressed against my eyes.

"Tell me what's going on, Redmond." Victor appeared in front of me and his hands gripped my shoulders.

"She...got into trouble and the school..." I could hardly form sentences, one thought monopolizing all others. "I can't lose her. I can't."

Victor gave my shoulders a shake. "Load up the car. I'm going to make a call. Be ready to go when I'm done."

I nodded and took a deep breath before standing on wobbly legs. I threw all my trust on him. Victor would know what to do. Victor would fix it. Victor would take care of everything. I had to believe that, despite everything, or fall apart entirely.

Victor disappeared into the back room while I cleaned up the kitchen and loaded up our bags. His voice, forceful and confident, leaked out in snatches and I tried not to imagine the other side of the conversation. I had just slammed the trunk closed when he rejoined me outside, a scowl on his face.

"She got into a physical altercation with one of her classmates," he said.

I kicked the tire and cursed.

"I'm afraid there's not much I can do. They've agreed to hold off calling your father to give us time to get there, but it may not matter."

"Why?"

"Parent or guardian, Redmond," he said gently. "From a legal standpoint, you are neither."

*Are you her legal guardian?*

Victor caught me by the elbows as I started to crumble again. He opened the passenger door and dropped me into the seat.

"Is there someone you can call?"

"It doesn't matter. Like you said—"

"I mean, for you."

Sean's face flashed in my mind. I ached to talk to him, to hear his easy laugh that made the world right even as it collapsed in on me.

"Yeah," I croaked.

"Okay. Good." He reached out his hand as if to touch my hair and then pulled back. He shuffled his feet and frowned. "I'll...give you a minute."

He disappeared back into the house. I just sat there, staring at the pavement between my feet before I finally gathered the courage to pull out my phone. I leaned forward with my elbows on my knees, forehead resting on the heel of my hand as it rang.

"Hey, stranger! Did you catch a big one?" Sean laughed. "By big one, I mean a fish."

At the sound of his voice, all barriers came crumbling down. My throat constricted around a sob, my breath escaping in shaky gasps.

"Whoa, what's going on?"

"I screwed up."

"What happened?"

"I lied to you," I said, tears dripping off the end of my nose. "You're my best friend, probably the only real friend I've had in a long time, and I keep lying to you. And I don't know why except that I'm scared. Scared of losing you. Of what you'll think of me. Because I need you. My life was shit before I met you."

"You need to start making sense, Red, because you're freaking me out."

"I'm not in Houston hanging out with a bunch of auto mechanics."

"Okay..."

"I'm in Galveston. With Victor."

A beat. "Oh."

"I didn't tell you because I knew you wouldn't approve—"

"You're goddamn right."

"—but I need your help." My voice cracked and tears burned my eyes again. "I need you to be my friend for one more day."

I didn't breathe in the silence that followed. There was a click on the other end of the line, and I pictured him chewing on the edge of his thumbnail.

"If you need me to bury a body, I'm out."

"It's my sister."

"You killed your sister? That's intense."

"No." Leave it to Sean to make me laugh when I'm falling apart. "She got into trouble in school. She got suspended."

"So, what, you need me to pick her up?"

"It's not that simple." I paused, heart racing. "They called our dad."

A sharp intake of breath. "Shit."

"We're leaving now, but—"

"It's okay, Red," he said quickly. "I'll go. I can be in Longview in an hour."

"They won't let you take her out."

"Well, maybe if I see your dad, I can run interference or something until you get here."

I released a long breath and my heart settled back into a less jerky rhythm. "Fuck. Thank you." I wiped my face and sat up straight. "Are you mad at me?"

"Of course, I'm mad at you. But this isn't about you and me right now, is it?"

I flinched at the sharpness of his words.

"Just get here safe, okay?"

"Okay."

Victor appeared at the end of the driveway just as I clicked off. "Ready to go?"

"Yeah." I swiveled around to face the windshield as Victor slid into the driver's seat. "I called Sean."

His jaw clenched and his hands tightened around the steering wheel. "I thought you might."

# Chapter 21

We made it to Longview in record time. The air between Victor and me was solid with things unsaid, but all I could think about was getting to Katie before the Colonel got there. Victor could have easily used this opportunity to punish me, but instead he just kept his eyes forward and his foot on the gas and two and a half hours later, we were rounding the corner to Oak Forest Charter School.

My jaw dropped when I saw it. Katie's description hadn't prepared me for the red brick and granite structure before me. It looked more like an Ivy League university than a high school. The main building was situated on a hill with a wide staircase that led up to the double doors. Statues in flowing robes flanked the entrance, eyes raised to the sky, and lions perched on the roof with their fangs bared, roaring at some invisible enemy. The kind of place you read about in books or saw in movies but never thought of as real.

I spotted his truck the moment we pulled into the parking lot. The big, black Chevy Silverado cast a dark shadow over a sea of luxury sedans. He'd had some version of the same truck for as long as I could remember, and it triggered a sick feeling. We'd hardly spoken more than ten words at a time to each other since I moved out. I embarrassed him and despite how much I hated him, it made something inside me bleed.

"He's here."

Victor slid the BMW into a parking space and cut off the engine. I crumpled forward in my seat, forehead against the dash. My hands shook, and I squeezed them between my knees as I took long breaths to compose myself. I had to be strong. For Katie and for myself. I couldn't let him break me down.

Victor laid his hand on my back. "Are you okay, Redmond?"

"No," I answered between gritted teeth. "I am most definitely not okay."

"Would you like me to go in with you?"

I shook my head.

"You sure?"

"It's not your job to take care of me, anymore."

He pulled his hand back with a sharp inhale and when I raised my eyes, there it was. That hurt I'd been looking for. But there was no satisfaction in it.

*One crisis at a time, Red.*

I swung the door open and slid out of the car. The rumble of the Chevy's engine vibrated the otherwise quiet afternoon air. A silhouette moved inside, and I strode toward it. Katie's mother sat in the passenger seat with the visor down, touching up her makeup and tucking stray hairs back into her auburn bun. She jumped when I tapped my knuckles on the glass.

"Redmond!" She smiled as she rolled down the window, though her lips were tight. "So good to see you."

"Is he here?"

Her smile faltered. "Oh, I just want to thank you so much for taking care of our girl these past few years—"

"Is. He. Here." I clenched my fists as my heart pounded a bruising rhythm against my sternum.

"Well, yes, he's—"

She gestured toward the building and I took off like a shot, taking the steps three at a time. I slowed as his imposing frame came into view just outside the double doors. The high-and-tight haircut, his square shoulders, his straight back. The unmistakable posture of a military man down to the crease in his slacks.

Colonel Cecil Redmond Cole, Navy Retired.

My feet froze on the top step. My chest filled with concrete. His back was to me, but his glare burned across my skin like a laser. My vision blurred, and I gripped the handrail as I struggled to breathe. My whole body screamed retreat until I heard a familiar voice talking the thickest line of bullshit I've ever heard.

Sean Delaney.

The tension drained out of me so fast I nearly fell down the stairs and I had to clap a hand over my mouth to stop the giddy laugh bubbling up from inside me. How many times had he saved me now just by being present?

"You're a military man, aren't you, sir? I mean, you look like a military man." Sean gesticulated wildly in an effort to keep the Colonel's attention, his cheeks pink and eyes wide. "We have a wonderful NROTC program and we are looking for boosters to help support—"

"I'm not interested, son," the Colonel replied in his typical condescending tone. "Now, if you please—"

He tried to sidestep around Sean who countered with a move of his own. They could have been dancing and the image had me fighting hysterics.

"But, sir, if I could just have a moment..." Sean trailed off as I stepped up onto the landing. A wash of emotions passed over his face—relief, disappointment, anger—and I had to look away or I would throw myself down at his feet.

The Colonel caught his eyeline and his head jerked in my direction. Only one expression hardened his brow: disgust.

"Redmond."

I jerked at the sound of his voice, stern and devoid of warmth. My back pulled straight, an instinctual response to a lifetime of swats across the shoulders and jabs in the ribs to correct my posture. I wanted to respond, but my throat clamped down and my tongue refused to move. His mouth twisted into a smirk and he jabbed his thumb over his shoulder toward Sean.

"*Friend* of yours?"

That familiar shame ripped through me and my skin burned as if I'd been doused in gasoline and he'd tossed a match, followed hard upon by rage. Rage at what he'd done to me, at the control I'd allowed him to have over my life.

Not anymore.

Without a word, I pushed past him and through the double doors. Inside, the school was much like any other. Long hallways lined with lockers stretched into the distance to my left and right. Trophies celebrating sports teams and academic achievements shone from behind glass. A wide common area opened out in front of me, filled with the smell of greasy pizza and pre-pubescence.

I spotted a sign pointing to the main office and took off down the hall at a full sprint. The Colonel's booming voice echoed off the walls, but I didn't stop. I knew he wouldn't chase, it would be beneath him, yet the image of his purposeful walk sent a chill up my back as if I were being followed by some horror movie monster.

I skidded to a stop in front of a bank of windows flanking a narrow wooden door. I could just see a line of desks through the blinds, manned by a team of stern women scowling at piles of paperwork. Their eyes jerked up as I burst through the door, panting like a marathon runner.

"I'm here...for Kaitlyn—"

"Red!"

Katie appeared from somewhere and threw her arms around my neck. Tears fell from eyes already puffy from crying.

"They called Dad," she said, voice muffled as she pressed her face into the crook of my neck.

"I know. He's here."

She clung to me tighter. "I'm so sorry, Red."

"Excuse me, sir." One of the women stood from behind her desk, wildly curly hair framing her round face like a lion's mane. "Can I help you?"

"I'm here to pick up Katie," I said. Katie's grip on my neck loosened, but she stayed close, clinging to my side.

The woman's eyes narrowed. "Are you her father?"

"*I'm* her father."

My stomach dropped as the Colonel appeared in the doorway, filling the entire office with his ominous presence. Katie whimpered against my shoulder and I wrapped my arms tight around her. The temperature in the room dropped as he raked his eyes over us.

"Let's go, Kaitlyn," he said with a jerk of his head.

"No."

His jaw tightened. "Excuse me?"

"I'm not going with you." Her fingers tightened around my arm, but she stood tall and her voice never wavered.

"Listen here, young lady. I've allowed the two of you to play house long enough—"

He took a step toward us and I pushed Katie behind me. "Don't touch her." My voice wasn't as steady as hers and it brought a slow smile to the Colonel's face.

"Miss, would you please call security," he said, cocking his head toward the frightened secretary. "This man is trying to kidnap my daughter."

My insides twisted as the secretary scrambled for the phone. "Why are you doing this?" I asked from between clenched teeth.

"Because Kaitlyn needs discipline. Something you are obviously lacking—"

"Oh, fuck you," I snarled. "If you gave a shit about her, you would have been banging down my door the day she ran away."

"Maybe I should have." His mouth twisted and he rocked forward on the balls of his feet. "But instead, I decided to have faith in you, Redmond."

His words sucked the air from my lungs. Despite the lifetime of manipulation and abuse, something glowed inside me at the prospect of his approval.

"But once again you've proven yourself not man enough for the challenge." His lips curled and his eyes narrowed. "Not surprising given your...*affliction*."

That pressure cooker inside me exploded, releasing every foul and loathsome thing he'd ever said to me. *Disgusting. Pervert. Fag.* Screamed behind blows. Hissed from between clenched teeth. In bright-yellow spray paint across the hood of a blue Prius. Bile rose in the back of my throat and vision went black around the edges.

"There is nothing wrong with me."

Katie yelped and the office ladies screamed as I lunged forward and shoved the Colonel hard in the chest. He let out a dull *oomph* as he tumbled backward out the door. His back slammed against the lockers on the opposite wall. For a moment, I just stood in the doorway, equal parts terrified and empowered by what I had done. He had always seemed so strong to me, an impenetrable fortress, but I had knocked him back.

He straightened slowly, lips curled and fire in his eyes, and I launched myself at him again. This time, he was ready for me. With a quick sidestep, he dodged and used my own momentum to slam me into the lockers. My teeth clashed together, and my head spun. He leaned his full weight against my back, grinding my cheek against the metal.

"You think you're tougher than me, boy?"

Katie came careening through the office door and threw herself at his back, punching and clawing. His weight shifted enough for me to get leverage to push away from the wall. Blind to everything but him, deaf to everything but Katie's cries, I spun around with my fist cocked.

A uniformed arm caught me before I could get it around. I released an animalistic growl as a pair of security guards restrained me and pulled me away from the Colonel. He had Katie by the arm, crying and digging in her heels as he tried to pull her down the hall.

"Take your hands off her," I choked, my throat closed with panic.

"Sir, I need you to calm down," said the burly guard wrapped around my right arm.

"I will not calm down until he takes his hands off my sister."

"What is the meaning of this?"

Everyone froze as Victor's sharp, cool voice cut through the chaos. He stood just down the hall, back straight, hands clasped behind his back. He pinned each man with an icy glare, eyes warming only when they fell on me.

"Who are you?" asked the guard.

"My name is Victor Itachi. I'm Mister Cole's lawyer."

The Colonel perked up. "You're not my—"

"The *other* Mister Cole."

I stared open mouthed as he stepped purposefully into the crowd, his back to the Colonel.

"Please, release my client."

The guards glanced at each other, brows furrowed. "We can't do that, sir. He attacked this man—"

"Did he?" Victor's eyes narrowed to slits and the guard flinched. "Yet, he's the only one with injuries."

Only then did I notice the throbbing over my right eye from where my head connected with the lockers.

"But—"

"Are you police or private security?"

"Private."

"Have the police been called?"

"N-no."

"Good." He inhaled deeply through his nose and pulled his shoulders back a notch. The guards traded a confused look again before loosening their grip enough for me to shrug out of it. I flexed my shoulders and spat a few curses before turning my glare back on my father. I stepped forward and Victor stopped me with a hand on my chest.

"Stay, Redmond."

My jaw tensed and my hands curled into fists, but I obeyed. The corners of his mouth twitched upward before he turned to face the others.

"Mister Cole."

"Colonel," he barked.

"Sorry?"

He lifted his head just enough to glare down his square nose. "I am a colonel in the United States Navy."

"Thank you for your service."

I'd never heard a thank-you sound so much like "fuck you" in my life.

"And you must be Kaitlyn."

Kaitlyn blinked back tears, recognition flashing over her face. She whimpered a bit, her arm still held fast in the Colonel's grip.

"Your client," my father started, "is trying to abduct my daughter."

"It's not true—" Katie's pleas were cut off by a jerk on her arm and I had to bite the inside of my cheek to keep still.

"It seems she doesn't want to go with you."

"She's sixteen, a minor, and it's not her decision."

"That's true." My stomach dropped. "But it's my understanding that up to today she's been living with her brother, Redmond."

"What's that got to do with—"

"And has been living there for some time." He leaned forward on the balls of his feet. "Did you make any effort to collect her, then? Or even contact her?"

The Colonel's face twisted but he remained silent.

"You're right, Colonel. You are within your rights as a parent to take Kaitlyn home. But, given the circumstances and her...duress—" Victor paused, his hands moving from behind his back to his hip pockets. "—you could expect a custody suit."

The Colonel took a step toward Victor. "He is unfit."

Victor met his glare. "And why is that, exactly?"

My mouth went dry. It was a dare. Daring him to say the thing he didn't want to admit in front of all these people. His face writhed with indecision as he fixed his laser beam eyes on me. They used to cut me. Now, I didn't even care.

Without a word, he dropped his hand from around Katie's arm and stepped back. Katie released a cry and flung herself into my arms, knocking me to my knees. I wrapped her up tight, face buried in her hair, eyes squeezed shut against the tears burning behind them. I didn't want to fall apart, not here in front of him, but I couldn't stop shaking.

I don't know how long we sat like that. I vaguely remember the distinct click of the Colonel's shoes walking away. Then, Victor's hand on my back.

"We should go, Redmond," he said gently.

I nodded and Katie and I stood without letting go of each other. The office ladies peered at us through the blinds as Victor ushered us back toward the front doors. I stopped short when we hit the outside landing. My fragile heart shuddered as my eyes whipped over the parking lot just in time to see a blue Prius pull out and speed away.

## Chapter 22

Victor's car was whisper quiet on the drive back to Black Creek. Katie sat in the back seat with her backpack clutched to her chest, wide eyes bouncing between Victor and me. Questions buzzed in the air like flies and we ducked our heads to avoid them until the familiar pop of a gravel driveway drowned them out.

Katie gasped as we pulled around that old plantation house where I'd left my truck. "Is this your house?" she asked, leaning forward to peer out of the windshield.

Victor laughed softly. "No."

"Whose is it?"

"Why don't you go wait in the truck?" I said, handing my keys back to her. She took them hesitantly, mouth half open as if she wanted to protest. Her eyes jerked between Victor and me again before she finally slid out of the back seat. She stopped and stuck her head back in.

"Does this mean I have to go back to public school?"

She looked at Victor, her eyes wide and tremulous, and my throat tightened. "I'm sorry, kiddo, but I don't think—"

"Of course, you don't have to go back to public school," Victor interjected with a soft smile. "I think we're all allowed one mistake."

"Victor, you don't have to—"

"I'm not in the habit of taking back gifts once given," he said sternly. "Kaitlyn's scholarship will be there for her for as long as she wants it."

Katie's eyes brightened. With a quick thank-you, she closed the door and skipped around to my truck. I didn't speak until the door slammed shut.

"Thank you," I said, croaking around the lump in my throat. "For what you did today."

"You don't have to thank me."

"Yes, I do. After everything—"

"I should have kissed you."

I blinked. "What?"

"Last night. In the bar." He tightened his grip around the steering wheel, his gaze fixed to the house in front of us.

I laughed despite the tears pushing against the back of my eyes.

"Can I call you?" He turned to face me and the sincerity in his eyes made my chest ache.

"I don't think so."

"So, this is really it, then?"

I nodded. "Yeah."

He released a long breath before facing back forward, eyes back on the building in front of us. It looked different somehow. Maybe it was the daylight. Maybe it was what I had found there. I reached over and squeezed Victor's knee.

"Goodbye, Victor."

The trunk popped as I exited the car and I transferred my bag into the bed of the pickup. I hesitated with my hand on the door, watching Victor's BMW kick up a trail of white dust as it pulled away. Katie watched me closely from the passenger side as I pulled myself up into the cab and sank into the seat.

"You okay?" she asked.

I closed my eyes for a moment. "Yeah, I think so. You?"

"Think so." She chewed her bottom lip and toyed with one of the straps on her bag. "Am I in trouble?"

"Are you ever going to fight in class again?"

She shook her head emphatically.

"Then, I think we're good."

She let out a breath and relaxed into the seat. I steeled myself for what came next as she poked at a worn patch of upholstery with her shoe.

"So...Victor Itachi..." Her voice cracked and she swallowed hard around it. "You're not just friends...are you?"

I let my head fall back onto the headrest. "No."

"That's why he was helping us?" I nodded and she laughed. "I knew there was a catch."

"It's not like that." She arched an eyebrow at me. I groaned and pressed the heels of my hands into my eyes. "It doesn't matter. I'm not going to see him anymore."

"Why not?"

"It's run its course."

"Did you love him?"

I took a deep breath as warmth rose up in me. It may not have been true love or even a healthy one, but it was still there. The love of two men brought together by their mutual brokenness.

"Yes."

Her eyes glistened and she laid her hand on my arm. "Then, I'm sorry."

My throat tightened and I struggled to swallow. "You don't...think..."

"Think what?"

"That there's something wrong with me? That I'm gross or—"

"No."

The word came out sharp and without hesitation. I released a long breath, flicked the ignition, and the truck rumbled to life. As I eased us out of the drive, I felt a pang of sadness knowing I would never come back here again. Never follow Victor into our room that held so many of my secrets.

"You could have told me, you know." Katie sniffed and rubbed her nose.

"I know. I wanted to."

"So, why didn't you?"

"I was scared."

"Well, you don't have to be scared anymore, okay, because I'm on your side."

The words came out sharp and tinged with anger, but they soothed something deep in my soul. It didn't matter what I was. It didn't matter what the world thought that meant. I was her big brother.

I reached across and took her hand and she laced her fingers through mine. "I'm sorry. I should have known better."

Silence fell over the cab and when I looked over again, she was turned sideways in her seat, eyes wide and tearful, her bottom lip poking out.

"Why are you looking at me like my puppy just died?"

She sniffed and her chin wobbled. "You're such a good person, Red. I just want you to be happy."

Katie slid across the bench seat and I had to pull over as she wrapped her arms around me and crawled into my lap like a child. I stroked her hair as she cried into my neck, fighting back tears of my own. I realized all over again how close I'd come to losing her and it made me shake.

"Hey, come on," I said with a wet laugh. "You don't have to worry about me. I'll get there, you know. I'm...getting there."

"I'm sorry I'm such a pain in the a—in the butt."

"You're my little sister. I think it's in the job description."

"I'm gonna be better, I promise."

"Me too. No more secrets. Because we're a team, right?"

She lifted her head and smiled. "Right. Love you, brother."

"Love you too, kiddo."

*  *  *

I expected to come home and find everything different. To find the sofa on the ceiling and the tub on the porch. But the world hadn't actually turned upside down. The house was just as I left it, with the exception of a Katie-level mess in the kitchen. The mailman still came every day. The sun still went up and down. The natural order intact.

The world hadn't changed. I had changed.

I went to work the next day feeling light. I still wasn't *out*, but I no longer felt like I was hiding, no longer carried the burden of shame. I worked harder, laughed easier. I'd spent so much of my life overanalyzing every word and action for fear of being discovered I forgot how much I truly loved working on cars. I even started working on my old Challenger again and freedom had never been so in reach. Only one thing stood in my way.

Sean.

I waited two days before I called him. I sat in the cab of my truck during my lunch break, sweating from more than just the heat, agonizing over what I would say. Though I did still feel the occasional pangs for my relationship with Victor, my friendship with Sean was by far my biggest loss, my biggest regret. I wanted more than anything to make it right.

I took one last breath and called up his name on my cell phone. I knew he wouldn't answer, but the sound of his voicemail message still gave me a sting. Curt and impersonal.

*"This is Sean. Leave a message."*

I cleared my throat. "Hey, Sean. It's me. Red." Heat crept up my neck and I scratched at my hairline. "Look, I know you're probably still mad at me. You should still be mad at me. I just wanted you to know how fucking amazing you are—" My teeth snapped down around the words too late and I punched the steering wheel. "I mean, what you did for me and my sister. That was amazing. Staring down the Colonel like that was just..."

I squeezed my eyes shut and leaned forward on the steering wheel. God, I was making a mess of this.

"Thank you. That's what I meant to say. And I'm sorry for... everything. I could make a hundred lame excuses for my behavior, but in the end, I just fucked up a good thing, and..." My throat constricted and my eyes burned. "I know you don't want to talk to me, you need time or whatever, so I won't call again. But I really hope you call me back. I miss you."

I clicked off and tossed the phone onto the seat next to me. The admission left me raw. I did miss him. God, did I miss him. And not just since that mess at the school. I'd missed him every time I'd lied to him, every time I'd pulled away because I was scared of him. I missed him sitting on that pier in Galveston with a man I could never truly be with. I must have thought of him a hundred times in the past two days, far more than I ever thought about Victor, and the thought of a life without him in it made me queasy.

I leaned back in my seat, eyes raised to the sky as if in prayer. "Please, call me back."

\* \* \*

A week passed. Then two. Katie went back to school and life carried on relatively normally. I worked on the Challenger every spare second I had, as much to keep my mind occupied as anything else. Rather than check my phone a hundred times a day for a call I was increasingly convinced would never come.

I'd put the new engine in and all that was left was some tuning and new fluids. Katie watched from a lawn chair in the driveway as

I topped up the oil and coolant, squinting into the compartment in search of leaks. A few last-minute checks and she was ready.

"Well, I think that's it." I wiped my hands on a rag and stretched my back with a satisfying crack. "Should we give her a try?"

Katie popped up out of her chair with a wide smile and slid into the passenger side. The car still needed a lot of cosmetic work, and she laid a shop towel on the seat to keep the cracked leather from biting into her legs.

"We should do a countdown like they do for the space shuttle," she said with a little wiggle.

"This is hardly a space shuttle."

"Oh, come on, Red. Where's your sense of adventure?" She slapped her hands on the dash, sending up a cloud of dust. "You've been working on this car practically your whole life. What's wrong with a little ceremony?"

A grin pulled at my lips and I rolled my eyes. "Okay, fine."

Katie squealed with glee and clapped her hands. "Yes! Okay, start from ten. Ready?"

I sat up straight, hands poised on the key in the ignition, as Katie began her countdown. As she gradually wound down to one, I thought of everything I'd gone through to get here. Leaving home young, scraping out a meager living, confronting and accepting my sexuality. Not to mention raising a pretty badass kid. I'd earned this. Earned my freedom with the blood of my knuckles and the sweat of my brow.

"*Blastoff!*" we shouted in unison. I twisted the key and the engine roared to life.

Katie whooped and pumped her fists in the air. Pure joy flooded my every cell as I eased the car out of the garage, and she purred like a contented cat in the sun. Oxidized paint that was once black was now a mottled gray, but she was still the most beautiful thing I'd ever seen.

I cut off the engine and sank back into the seat with a sigh. It was perfect. Almost.

"You should call him."

I flinched. "What? Who?"

She clicked her tongue and gave me an *oh, please* look. As part of my new policy of openness, I'd told her all about Sean and our ill-fated friendship. First, she'd hugged me. Then, she called me an asshole and punched me in the arm hard enough to bruise. She wasn't wrong.

I groaned and scrubbed at the space between my eyebrows. "I can't."

"Why not?"

"Because I said I wouldn't."

She rolled her eyes. "Okay, so go see him." She flashed a sly grin and bounced her eyebrows. "There's no way he can resist you in your hot new car."

"Give me a break." I laughed, but my hands tightened on the steering wheel.

Her expression softened. "Seriously though. Odds are the only reason he hasn't called is he's as scared as you."

"I'm not—" She cut me off with another roll of her eyes. "Look, that whole 'camp out in front of your crush's house' thing only works in rom-coms. In real life, it's grounds for a restraining order."

"I'm not saying be creepy. But maybe if he's somewhere...and you happen to be there too..."

"That's not creepy?"

She shrugged. "Not if he wants to see you."

I blew out a breath. "Sounds like a big risk."

"Yeah." She leaned over and squeezed my arm. "But at least you'll know."

# Chapter 23

T he Challenger rocked and complained as I navigated it through the trees to the river's edge, my heart lodged firmly behind my larynx. Part of me hoped the clearing would be empty and sweat broke out along my hairline as Sean's blue Prius came into view. He'd backed up to the waterline and sat on the trunk, feet perched on the bumper and a fishing pole hanging loosely from his fingers.

He pivoted on his hip as I rumbled into the clearing and parked beside him, one brow cocked as he studied the unfamiliar vehicle. They lowered when he spotted me through the windshield and his lips pressed into a thin line.

I took a deep breath before opening the door and stepping out. My car sat between us and I rested my elbows on the top.

"Hey."

"Hey." His eyes drifted over the car and then back to me. "New project?"

I shrugged. "Old one, actually. Just got it running. It's sort of a metaphor for my whole life."

One corner of his mouth twitched upward before settling into a hard line again. "What are you doing here, Red?"

"Wanted to see you."

He inhaled as if to speak but stayed silent. He turned to face the water again. His grip tightened around the rod, but he made no indication he wanted me to leave. I circled around the cars to stand beside him, leaning on the back of the Prius, eyes on the orange light bouncing off the water.

"Did you get my message?"

"Yeah, I got it," he answered without looking at me.

"Good." I kicked at the rocks, the silence between us so hard not even the birds could break through it. "I came out to my sister."

His brows lifted and his eyes cut toward me.

"She wasn't as bothered as I would have thought." I laughed and scratched at the back of my neck. "Turns out she just wants me to be happy."

"That's good, Red." He nodded and his eyes dropped back to his lure. I missed his eyes and how he used to look at me, so honest and open.

"Sometimes, I wish I hadn't met you."

His back jerked straight and his jaw dropped. Hurt flared in his eyes as he pivoted to face me, and I raised my hand as if to fend off blows.

"That's not what I meant. Just hear me out, okay."

"This better be good."

I lowered my hands, taking a moment to gather my thoughts. "I wish I hadn't met you *then*," I said carefully. "When we met, I was confused, scared. I was so fucking scared. I know that's no excuse, but..."

Sean's posture softened a bit and I continued. "I've learned a lot about myself since I met you. Addressed some things I'd let fester for far too long. I know myself better, now. I know who I am, who I want to be. I'm not scared anymore."

My heart had dislodged from my throat and now flopped around in my chest like a landed fish. "What I mean to say is, I wasn't ready for you. I wish I could meet you now. Now that I'm not such a fucking mess. Now that I can be open with you in all the ways you deserve. I wish we could start over. Can't we just start over?"

His eyes trembled before dropping to the ground. "It doesn't work like that, Red."

"Why not?"

"Because you hurt me." He slapped the trunk and the whole car shook. "I thought we were friends."

"We were friends."

"No. I was your friend. You weren't mine."

I reeled as if he'd slapped me. He wasn't wrong. He'd been open with me from the start. Allowed me into his life when he knew nothing about me. Bared his pain to me. Comforted me when my life spiraled out of control. And all I'd done was hide, putting public perception ahead of our relationship.

"I'm sorry." My voice cracked. I'd never been so cowed.

"How many times have you apologized to me, Red?" His eyes welled and his voice shook. "Apologies are meaningless if your behavior doesn't change."

I stood up straighter. "I have changed."

"I can't trust you." A tear dropped and he turned his face away.

"Sean—"

"Please leave."

My glass heart cracked under his words. My mouth went dry. All this time, I'd been nursing a flicker of hope he could forgive me. As I stumbled back to my car, it went out in a puff of smoke, leaving an empty space behind.

By the time I got home, I'd gone completely numb. Katie jumped up from the couch when I walked in, the textbook that had been open on her lap sliding to the floor. Her wide-eyed expression fell when she saw my face.

"Well..." I said with a broken shrug. "At least I know."

* * *

I couldn't sleep. The numbness had worn off, replaced by a deep ache that left me tossing and turning until I'd become so tangled in my sheets I couldn't move anymore. I kept seeing the image of Sean's silhouette disappearing against the darkness as I pulled away. I replayed our conversation over and over in my head, thinking of all the things I could have said differently as if some magic spell existed that could restore our friendship, and all I had to do was find it.

Around 1:00 a.m. I gave up. I threw my bedclothes across the room with a growl and stomped into the kitchen. I squinted into the glowing belly of the refrigerator until I saw spots, ultimately grabbing the gallon of milk and a box of cereal from the cupboard.

I had just poured the milk over my frosted flakes when I heard a buzzing from the living room. My phone glowed from the coffee table, and my stomach twisted. Only one person ever called me this late. An itch started between my shoulder blades, and my mouth went dry. A silent command of *heel* vibrated through my bones. I drifted through the dark toward the phone, blinking at its pulsing face.

Sean.

I snatched up the phone and jabbed the accept button. "Hey."

Silence.

"Sean?" I glanced at the phone's screen. Had I hung up on him by mistake?

"I miss you too."

My whole body turned to jelly, and I sank to the couch with a loud groan.

"This doesn't mean I'm not mad at you."

"I know."

"I'm serious, Red. This is the last fucking time."

"I hear you." My heart pounded so hard, I felt it in my toes. "I'll be better. I promise."

"Okay." The word came out an exhale and the silence that followed was considerably softer than the ones preceding it. "So... now what?"

"We start over, I guess."

"Right." When he spoke again, there was a smile in his voice. "Do you fish?"

# Chapter 24

So, we started over. Sean and I went fishing the very next evening and it became a sort of standing date. No matter what happened in our lives, we always made time to go fishing until it became part of our shorthand. I'd roll up his long drive in my pickup and he'd be there waiting, two poles and a tackle box in hand, and every time felt like winning the lottery.

Every day I worked hard to earn back his trust. He kept me at arm's length at first, which broke my heart a little, but I understood it. While I wasn't what you would call *out* to anyone outside my family, I didn't hide either. He would occasionally meet me at work on my lunch break. Instead of panicking about being seen with him, I'd drop the tailgate of my truck, and we'd share fast food burgers right there in the parking lot. A small gesture, but I knew it meant a lot and little by little, the wall between us came down until we were practically inseparable.

"God damn, Red." Sean leaned back in his chair with a contented groan and rubbed his belly. "That might just be the best steak I've ever had."

I laughed as I reached across the table to clear his plate. Katie was spending the night with friends in Longview and I'd taken the opportunity to invite him over for dinner. Steaks off the grill, loaded baked potatoes, and grilled asparagus smothered in garlic. His face lit up with every bite and I might have taken more pleasure in watching him eat than in the steak itself.

"It's sort of my specialty," I said proudly, pausing at the sink. "Sure you don't want to lick the plate?"

"Don't tempt me."

I gave the plates a rinse, dropped them in the dishwasher, and grabbed a couple of beers before heading back to the table. I spun mine between my fingers as Sean took a deep pull and released a sigh of pleasure.

"Do you remember," I started, my heart in my throat, "the night I came out to you?"

"Of course I do." He laughed. "God, we got so drunk. I think I'm still hung over."

"Yeah." I shifted in my seat and scratched at the back of my neck. "You told me you had a crush on me."

His smile flickered and a trickle of dread ran down my spine. He laughed again, tighter than before. "I think that might have been the tequila talking."

"Maybe." I took a long swig of my beer. "Thing is, I might have a crush on you too."

Sean froze, his beer bottle pressed against his lips.

"I think we should go on a date."

He lowered the bottle back down to the table and his focus went hazy.

"Come on, man, say something." I laughed in an attempt to lighten the mood. "Even if it's to tell me to fuck off. I'm kind of dying over here."

His eyes snapped back into focus and the corners of his mouth pulled up. "Okay."

My heart leaped. "Okay?"

He gave a one-shouldered shrug and a nod as he sipped his beer.

"Okay." I blew out a breath. "So...what do you want to—"

"What if it's this?"

I blinked. "What do you mean?"

"What if this is our first date?" He smiled and his eyes sparkled. "A couple of beers. An amazing meal. It's a pretty good start if you ask me."

"Well, you might be disappointed in the end, because I don't have anything planned after the steaks."

"You have Netflix? I've never seen *Inception*. I hear the twist ending is killer."

"Yeah. Sure. Okay."

Sean got up and moved to the couch. I followed behind him, a little punch-drunk. *Is this a date? Are we dating?* My cheeks burned as I fumbled with the remote. For some reason, all I could think about was all that garlic on the asparagus.

"That's it," Sean said as the thumbnail flashed on the screen.

I called it up and settled back into the couch as the movie started rolling. The iconic soundtrack filled the room and I suddenly didn't know what to do with myself. I squirmed in my seat, tapped my foot, picked at a hole in my jeans. God, our first date and I was dressed like a goddamned hobo.

*For fuck sake, just watch the movie.*

I willed myself to relax and within a few minutes, I was totally absorbed until I felt a warmth against my side. Sean had shimmied up close to me, his legs tucked up beneath him. I lifted my arm to the back of the couch and he tucked himself underneath it, resting his head on my shoulder. His hair smelled lightly floral and it released a swarm of fireflies in my chest.

As the movie wound on, I found myself continuously distracted by all the little things I'd never noticed. The way his hair curled around his ears. The gentle slope of his spine. The way he flexed his feet when he got restless. Things I was sure I'd seen but had somehow missed their importance. I let my fingers drift over his collarbone, and he released a shuddering breath.

"Everything okay?"

"Yeah." He sniffed and wiped his nose with the back of his hand.

"Sean."

"I'm fine, Red." He tensed, but didn't move, his fingers bunching in my shirt. A few seconds later, he lifted his face and his eyes shimmered. "You better not fucking hurt me."

The fireflies in my chest turned to bees, everything I'd done to put that doubt in his eyes delivering a sting. I cupped his face in my hand and ducked my head, aligning my lips with his and waiting, just waiting for him to close the distance. When he did, it felt like exploding into a million pieces and shooting into the stars.

I never did see that twist ending.

# About the Author

Courtney Maguire is a University of Texas graduate from Corpus Christi, Texas. Drawn to Austin by a voracious appetite for music, she spent most of her young adult life in dark, divey venues nursing a love for the sublimely weird. A self-proclaimed fangirl with a press pass, she combined her love of music and writing as the primary contributor for Japanese music and culture blog, Project: Lixx, interviewing Japanese rock and roll icons and providing live event coverage for appearances across the country.

Email: CourtneyMaguireWrites@gmail.com
Facebook: www.facebook.com/CourtneyMaguireWrites
Twitter: @PretentiousAho
Website: www.courtneymaguirewrites.com
Instagram: www.instagram.com/courtneymaguirewrites

# Coming Soon: Wounded Martyr
## Chapter One

Everything hurt.

Hiding in our dingy dressing room toilet, back pressed against the wall between the sink and the urinal, I read wall graffiti to take my mind off my sore joints. Black Sharpie marker slander tucked between worn band stickers. *Jake is a pussy. For a good time, call.* Someone had scrawled *SUX* over a Wounded Martyr sticker in the corner. An old one. Apparently, we'd played here before. I couldn't remember.

House music vibrated through the wall, and I pressed my shoulder blades into it. I gave a no-smoking sign the finger and pulled a pack of cigarettes out of my pocket. This used to be my favorite part, the anticipation in the moments before we hit the stage. Now, I shook with a mix of adrenaline and dread that made me queasy.

"Ice!" A familiar voice cut through the din followed by a rapid knock on the door. "Dude, you in there?"

I popped a cigarette between my lips. "Fuck off, I'm taking a shit."

The door opened anyway, and in slipped Ashton. *Ash.* Hair in his face and dark liner around his eyes. Deep lines framed his mouth, but his too-long limbs made him appear perpetually boyish. The way I would always see him. The sixteen-year-old kid playing bass in his garage.

"You can't smoke in here."

I scowled and shoved the cig back in the pack.

"Dante is going to lose his shit if you don't get out there," he said, closing the door behind him. Dante, our self-appointed fearless leader. If he wasn't such a goddamned great guitarist, I'd kick him in the teeth.

"Dante can suck my cock."

"Pretty sure he's not into that." We shared a laugh before his eyes pinched in concern. "How's the voice?"

"Tired," I answered on the tail end of an exhale.

"You can make it, man." He stepped toward me. "Just three more shows, and we're home."

"Have you seen the house?"

"Yeah."

"Is it full?"

He pressed his lips together, and those lines around his mouth deepened.

"Shit."

"Don't sweat it." He squeezed my arm. "It's a big house. It would be hard for anyone to fill. Besides, we've played smaller."

I nodded, but my stomach dropped into my toes. Sure, we'd played smaller. I remembered playing crowds of twenty people, ten of whom hated us. But we were eighteen with nowhere to go but up, and nothing to lose. It felt different now.

Ash's expression softened. "What do you need?"

A drink.

"A blow job from John Stamos."

"You and me both." He hooked his hand around the back of my neck and pressed our foreheads together. "You'll be great," he said. "You *are* great. Just another day at the office, man, you got this."

I leaned into him and released a long breath. Just another day. Another day I got to play rock and roll. Living the dream, most would say. But even dreams didn't last forever.

"What the fuck are you two doing in there? Put your dicks away, and let's go," Dante's gruff voice shouted from the other side of the door. Ash shot me a mischievous grin and dropped to his knees just as the door swung open. "What the fu—"

"Be right out, Boss," I said, but he'd already stomped off, spitting and cursing the whole way back to the dressing room, his bright copper skin dark with an angry flush. I gave Ash a kick with my heel, and he rolled over backward, tangled in his own legs and howling.

"Homophobes are fun," he said between gasps.

"You're a prick," I said, but I was smiling, my earlier dread carried away in the stream of his laughter. Dante had left the door open, and the house music pounded through me, ringing the tuning fork inside. It was still there, thank God. I offered Ash a hand and hauled him up.

"Ready to go?" he asked, his hand still wrapped in mine.

"Let's get to work."


Two hours later, I stumbled off the stage, aching and sweaty and completely empty. Barely a half-full house, but Ash was right. It didn't matter. They seethed and roared and filled the space with an energy that ignited my soul. For two hours, my exhaustion disappeared. I was a god and they worshipped me. In return for their love, I gave them everything, singing until my voice splintered, and in the end, I had to be carried off the stage.

Someone handed me a bottle of water, and I collapsed against the wall, slumped between a couple of equipment crates. The adrenaline fled fast, leaving my whole body screaming. I gulped down the water, and fire slid down my throat with every swallow. I tasted blood. Fuck.

Ash stumbled into my field of vision, equally destroyed, but he carried it differently. Like he welcomed it, was made for it. He peeled off his shirt, and his lean body gleamed in the dimness. Eyeliner ran in thick black streaks down his cheeks and left a dirty smudge on the towel he used to wipe his face. He threw his head back and laughed as our rhythm guitarist, Dai, ran up and slapped him on the back. It rang like bells through the hiss in my ears.

He spotted me in the dark and winked, sending a tendril of warmth through my sore muscles. Twenty years I'd known him, and I was still in awe of him.

He crouched down in front of me. "Told you you'd be great."

"Monitors were fucked," I grumbled. "I couldn't hear shit."

"I don't think anyone noticed."

"I noticed."

He laughed and shook his head, brushing off my foulness. "Ready to face the gauntlet?"

I groaned. "What if we slept here?"

"God, when did you turn into such a grouch?"

"Somewhere around thirty-five, I think."

"Well, come on, Oscar." He stood and pulled me up with him. I wobbled a little, and he tucked me close against his side, arm looped around my waist. "Let's get out of here."

After gathering up our personal belongings—the gear was someone else's job—we met the rest of our bandmates at the club's back door. Our drummer, Nate, the gentle giant, his hulking stature contradicted by a meek personality, eased the door open a crack. A high-pitched squeal cut through the air, and he snapped it shut again.

"I say we send Dai out first as a distraction," he said, his soft voice tremulous. Dai flashed a Cheshire cat grin and puffed out his chest.

"I offer myself as tribute." He ran a hand through his fire-engine red mane.

Dante rolled his eyes. "I'll get security."

"For fuck sake, can we just get this over with?" I barked.

"The van just pulled up," Nate said after another peek. "We can make it if we run."

We lined up in front of the door, faces grim like paratroopers preparing to drop into a warzone. Dai pushed through the door first. As predicted, the ladies in the crowd flocked to him, giving us an opening to run past and into the waiting passenger van. We tumbled over one another as we fought our way into the bench seats, and I landed squarely in Ash's lap.

"Daisuke!" Dante shouted out of the open door, but Dai had been swallowed by a sea of autograph seekers and cell phone cameras. Security finally appeared, herding the crowd with shouts and whistles and allowing Dai to back his way into the van.

"Shit, did you see that?" he said. "Those girls were on my dick like it was chocolate flavored."

"Not as many as the last time," Nate pointed out.

"Smaller crowd." The dark feeling snuck in again, making my voice thick. Ash laced his fingers through mine and squeezed.

Dante gave the order and the van pulled away, weaving through the throng. A short drive and another back entrance later, we were back at the hotel. It could have been a Four Seasons. It could have been a Holiday Inn. I couldn't tell anymore.

Dead on our feet, we snuck through the halls to the elevators.

"The bar's still open," Dai whooped, startling us awake. "Shots on me. Who wants 'em?"

Dante scowled. Nate mumbled something about sleep apnea and averted his eyes. I stiffened as his gaze landed on us.

"I can always count on you, Ash," he said with a beckoning wave. Ash sucked in a breath and glanced at me.

"What, do you need permission?" I snapped. "Just go."

His mouth twitched into a smile that set my teeth on edge before he loped off to join Dai. I wanted to join them, so bad I had to twist my muscles into knots to keep them still. I imagined the first shot going down like fire, the following like water. Felt the dreamy softness as they pushed the world a little further away.

This was not a good day for temptation.

Weariness hit hard when I finally made it to my room. The door clicked shut behind me, the particular click of a magnetic lock like a jail cell, and I leaned back against it. I closed my eyes, took a deep breath, and the dry air clawed at my lungs. The air of a place not really lived in, unwarmed by human presence. My ears still throbbed with the echoes of the show, and I pressed my fingers against them, but it only made it worse. There was nothing louder than the silence of an empty room.

A dark pit opened up inside me, and I grit my teeth against the vertigo. Soon, Ash would be in here with me. Maybe then it wouldn't feel so cold.

I dropped my knapsack in the entryway and stumbled into the room without bothering to turn on the lights. I curled up in my hard hotel bed and tried not to think about everything that had gone wrong. About a tour of half-filled venues and spitting blood. I buried my nose in my pillow and filled my head with technical things. Mics and speakers and amps. Chord progression and phrasing and the *thump thump thump* of a six-string bass.

It could have been seconds later. It could have been hours. I snapped awake to a weight in my bed and a long body pressed up against mine. Ash. Finally.

"What are you doing?" I growled as he slipped his arms around me.

"I'm tired." He smelled of stale cigarettes and cheap booze.

I wiggled in his grip and poked my elbow into his ribs. "Go to your own bed."

"My bed is too big for me," he whined, pressing his nose in the back of my neck.

"What are you, twelve?" I asked.

"Please please please let me stay." He hugged my waist as if the world itself might tip and throw him out of bed, and my resolve crumbled fast. I slid my hands over his forearms and held them. How long had it been since I'd had someone's arms around me?

"God, you're a clingy drunk."

"Better than a mean one." He gasped, and his body went rigid. "Shit. That wasn't—I didn't mean—"

Heat rushed to my face. My grip on his arms changed, and I flung them off me. "I'm mean sober too. Now, get out of my bed, and go the fuck to sleep."

He cursed under his breath, rolled away from me, and hit the ground with a heavy thud. I curled into a tight ball and pulled the covers up to my nose. Ash's unintentional dig stuck like an arrow in my back. He'd been there through it all. Watched me disintegrate into a seething pile of awfulness. Watched me struggle to piece the scraps back together. Two years sober and I was still struggling. Part of me wondered if he resented it. If he held onto some secret hope I would get better.

The scariest part about getting sober is finding out who you really are. Turned out I wasn't much different.

A panicked squeak pierced the dark followed by a crash. "What is going on over there?" I growled, flopping onto my back and stabbing on the light. When my eyes adjusted, I found Ash tangled up in his own shirt, arms straight up over his head and the fabric pulled tight over his face. He tossed himself around the room, bumping into furniture, knocking over lamps, and kicking over my suitcase as he struggled against it. I'd have been pissed if it wasn't so goddamn funny.

"For fuck sake," I said, pulling myself out of bed and grabbing hold of his shoulders.

"I'm stuck!"

"I see that. Hold still." I grabbed the wad of fabric bunched up under his chin. I worked it upward, revealing his pouting lips, his

217

scrunched-up nose, and nostalgia rushed through me for the snaggle-toothed kid I used to know. His crooked smile had been replaced by an uncanny valley of veneers. One of the first big purchases he'd made once we started making money. He should have bought a car.

"Why did you do that...to your teeth?"

"What, get them fixed?" he asked, shaking his hair as his head popped free, his arms still tangled in the air overhead.

"There was nothing wrong with them."

"I looked like a sewer rat." He tucked his bottom lip behind his upper teeth in a buck-toothed grimace.

I forced his elbows straight and worked his arms free. "I thought you were cute before."

"You don't think I'm cute now?" he asked with a cheeky grin.

"Sure, I do. It made me sad is all." I gave the shirt one final yank, and it came free. "Like you were listening to all those people."

"What people?" he asked, dropping his arms to his sides and rolling his shoulders in relief.

"All the ones telling you you weren't good enough." A rush of heat flooded my cheeks. He went very quiet, a strange, almost sad expression settling over his face.

"Who were you listening to?"

"When?"

"When you drank your first paycheck."

Touché.

"Probably the same people," I conceded. "Speaking of drinking too much, can you get out of your pants without killing yourself, or do you need help with that too?"

He frowned and yanked at his belt buckle, every ounce of attention on his fumbling fingers as he struggled with the latch. I sighed and batted them away. He rested his hands on my shoulders, and another wave of heat splashed over me as I eased his pants over his hips.

"I'm sorry," he said as I pushed him down on the edge of the bed, "for what I said before."

"I'm sorry too." I ducked my head and went down on my knees in front of him, cupping his calf in my hand as I guided his pants down his long legs. "For being mean."

He slid his hands up my neck, and my heart skittered as he curled his fingers in my short hair. The room wasn't cold anymore but superheated with his presence and a million unsaid things. He traced the shell of my ear and the line of my jaw, and I was too tired to bat him away. He whispered something that could have been my name, and when I lifted my face, his lips latched to mine, soft and whiskey-flavored. In twenty years, we'd shared hundreds of kisses. Quick, chaste things full of comfort and affection, but none like this.

I pulled away for half a second as logic tried to intervene, but like a magnet he drew me back again. His lips parted, pulling me in deeper, and I fell into him. He pulled me into the bed with him, and I had no choice but to follow, climbing his body until I covered it.

"Wait, Ash—" I tried to pull away again, making it less than a hair's breadth. "Fuck, you taste like whiskey."

He smiled against my lips. "You want to drink me?"

I groaned as he pushed his tongue against mine. "Stop. You're drunk."

"I know what I'm doing."

"We can't. I mean...we shouldn't..."

"I know. Fuck, I know," he said breathlessly. "But I really want to. Don't you want to?"

He pulled our hips together, lighting a fire under my skin. I tried to push him away. I tried, but it was as if our skin had melted together. No going back, no point in resisting. Forcing ourselves apart would only cause injury.